"How do y

"He's in my wa[...]

"*He's* the weirdo guy you were telling me about—the one who showed up late and then griped for the entire hour?" Kathy guffawed. "Why didn't you tell me?"

"Can I help it I have a problem with names?" Sailor crossed her arms. "So what's the big deal?"

Kathy shared a look with Audra. "Good grief, Sailor. Parker Travis is probably *the* most eligible bachelor in Birkenstock." Audra scooted onto the seat next to Kathy and clicked her enameled fake nails on the tabletop. "Not to mention he's one marvelous hairstylist."

"Well, he's a lousy student." Sailor looped her arm through the strap of her tan microfiber ergonomic purse and edged out of the booth. "I'll let you two dish the hairdresser. I've got to get back to the Y."

MYRA JOHNSON has roots that go deep into Texas soil, but she's proud to be a new Oklahoman. Myra and her husband have two married daughters and five grandchildren. Empty nesters now, they share their home with two lovable dogs and a snobby parakeet. *Autumn Rains*, Myra's first novel for Heartsong Presents, won the 2005 RWA Golden Heart for Best Inspirational Romance Manuscript.

Books by Myra Johnson

HEARTSONG PRESENTS
HP873—Autumn Rains

Romance by the Book

Myra Johnson

Heartsong Presents

For Julie Lessman, my favorite real-life Missouri author, and for Candy, the hairstylist who always makes me look my best!

A note from the Author:
I love to hear from my readers! You may correspond with me by writing:

Myra Johnson
Author Relations
PO Box 721
Uhrichsville, OH 44683

ISBN 978-1-60260-699-9

ROMANCE BY THE BOOK

Our mission is to publish and distribute inspirational products offering exceptional value and biblical encouragement to the masses.

PRINTED IN THE U.S.A.

one

"Is it in yet?" Sailor Kern stretched her thin frame across the library checkout counter. Her elbows dug into the yellow Formica. "*Please*, Kathy, tell me you have it."

The dark-haired woman behind the counter arched one eyebrow as she scanned the bar codes on a stack of returned books. "Have what?"

Sailor huffed. "Come *on*, Kathy. You're supposed to be my best friend. Don't keep me in suspense."

With infuriating slowness Kathy Richmond scanned another book and placed it on the rack behind her. "Are you referring to the new Chandler Michaels novel?"

"What else?" Sailor stood erect, one sneaker-clad foot tapping out her impatience. "You promised I was next on the waiting list."

An impish grin skewed Kathy's lips. She turned away and dug deep into the back of a filing-cabinet drawer, spun around with a flourish, and plopped a book on the counter. "Ta-da!"

Sailor snatched up the book and hugged it to her chest. "Do you have any idea how long I've been waiting to read this?"

"Seeing as how you've checked out every one of Chandler's fourteen previous books at least twice and have been bugging me about his latest release every day for the past month, I would say. . .yes." Kathy groaned and glanced toward the ceiling. "You could have picked up your own copy over at Dale & Dean's Book Corner the day it came in."

"Buy it? At hardcover price? Do I need to remind you what they pay me at the Y?" Sailor held the novel at arm's length and slid admiring fingertips across the slick, shiny book jacket. It pictured a raven-haired, Victorian-era songstress in the arms of her dashing hero. "*Love's Sweet Song*. This one has got to be his most tender romance yet—proof you don't need graphic love scenes to tell a great story."

"On that much, I can agree." Kathy motioned Sailor aside while she assisted an elderly library patron. She tucked the gentleman's receipt into the top book and pushed the stack toward him. Speaking slowly and distinctly, she said, "These are due back on the sixteenth, Mr. Crenshaw."

"Thanks"—Mr. Crenshaw squinted toward Kathy's chest—"Kandy. It's a date, sweetheart." With a wink he gathered up his books and headed toward the exit.

"What a flirt." Sailor planted one hip against the counter. "And did he just call you Kandy?"

"His eyesight's almost as bad as his hearing. You did notice everything he checked out was the large-print edition?"

"I also noticed his gaze lingered a bit longer than necessary on your, uh, name tag."

"He's a harmless old coot." Grinning, Kathy resumed her book scanning. "Besides, we thirty-something single girls have to take romance anywhere we can find it."

"Don't remind me." An old, familiar ache settled under Sailor's breastbone. Between her incurable shyness and ordinary looks, the only romance she could expect came from the pages of books like the one she held. She eyed the alluring songstress again and heaved an envious sigh before handing Kathy the book along with her library card.

"Oh, Sailor, I was kidding." Kathy checked out the book for her and then motioned one of the other librarians over to help the next patron. She stepped around the counter and gave Sailor's shoulder a squeeze. "I only get a half-hour lunch break today. Can you join me in the snack bar just this once? There's something I've been dying to talk to you about."

Kathy hummed softly, avoiding Sailor's probing gaze as they entered the glass-walled elevator that would whisk them to the lower level. Sailor's stomach twisted—and it had nothing to do with her noontime hunger pangs or the disgustingly fattening aromas of hot dogs and fries wafting their way. Nope, when Kathy Richmond got that look in her eye, it usually meant she was about to push Sailor way out of her comfort zone.

And it didn't take much.

૨૦

"Ow! That hurts, Doc!" Parker Travis cringed and ducked from beneath Andy Mendoza's probing fingers.

"Hold still, will you? How else do you expect me to diagnose your back pain?"

"X-rays. MRI. CT scan." Parker reached around to rub the sore spot behind his right shoulder.

"Man, what a hypochondriac." The doctor dug his thumbs deep into the center of Parker's aching back muscle, eliciting another yelp. "An X-ray or MRI isn't going to tell me anything I don't already know. This is clearly an overuse injury, probably from spending too many hours a day wielding a hair dryer."

"So you don't think it's anything serious?" Health issues always made Parker slightly nervous, especially since so many men on *both* sides of his family tree had died before age fifty. He wanted to be around to make sure his widowed mom and grandmother were well cared for as long as they lived.

"Nope, you're as healthy as a horse." Andy jotted notes in Parker's file. "Although maybe you should've chosen a different career. Not to mention how you have to twist your upper body to hold a flute."

Parker groaned at the reminder. On Sundays he and Andy played in their church's praise team band—Parker on flute and Andy on drums. But lately the sets had left Parker almost as crippled from pain as his salon work. "I love what I do. You expect me to give up the things I enjoy most?"

Andy took hold of Parker's arm, moving the shoulder through its range of motion. "Actually, being on your feet for hours at a time, I'm surprised you aren't complaining about your knees."

"Ouch! Will you stop that?" Parker almost wished he'd never made this appointment. Suffering in silence had to be easier than dealing with his old high school–band buddy's razzing. No way he'd admit to his chronic knee pain now, especially if the esteemed Dr. Andrew Mendoza had nothing more helpful to offer.

"Sorry, Park. Seriously, the best thing for you is a course of NSAIDs for the inflammation and some therapeutic exercise." He jotted something on a prescription pad.

"But I already work out. I run several days a week, do free weights in between."

"A regimen that only exacerbates your issues. The muscles have tightened up and need to be stretched." Andy perused the rack of health-related brochures mounted on the exam room door. He selected one and offered it to Parker. "Have you ever considered water aerobics?"

Only a know-it-all show-off like Andy would use words like *regimen* and *exacerbates*. Parker glimpsed the red and black symbol for the YMCA but kept his hands firmly planted beside his thighs. His grandmother and her friends at the assisted-living center did water aerobics. He loved those gals, but... "Can't you refer me to a physical therapist, or maybe a personal trainer?"

Andy smirked. "A bit image conscious, are we? Water aerobics is a great way to exercise without stressing the joints. Especially good for sore knees," he added with a wink. He tapped Parker's arm with the sharp edge of the brochure. "Sign up. Doctor's orders."

Parker slithered into his black polo shirt with the Par Excellence Salon and Day Spa logo embroidered on the breast pocket. He'd worked hard to get to this place in life, overcome a lot of kidding and even more innuendos. Male hairstylists, even guys like him who owned and managed their own salons, weren't exactly seen as the strong, macho type. Neither were closet hypochondriacs or men who played the flute. It didn't matter that he played on his church's men's softball team and could easily slug one over the fence. Didn't matter that his Birkenstock High 100-yard-dash record remained unbroken.

If folks around town found out he'd joined his grandmother's water aerobics class, the teasing would never end.

Later, pulling into a vacant space in front of the Willow Tree Assisted-Living Center, he'd about decided to call Andy again and insist on a referral to a specialist. If Birkenstock didn't have one, Springfield was just up the highway.

Then he reached into the backseat for his styling kit, and the stabbing pain in his back made him grab the door frame and suck in his breath.

Two hours and six little old ladies' gray heads later, he was ready to dress in tights and a pink tulle skirt if it would make the pain go away.

❧

Sailor sat in her cramped cubicle behind the YMCA reception area and paged through a stack of registration forms. Her introductory water aerobics class starting tomorrow looked to be an interesting group. A pair of sixty-something twins who were more than a tad overweight. A new mom hoping to return to her prepregnancy fitness level. A stressed-out paralegal. Three high school teachers who signed up together for fun. All women, of course. Never any cute guys. They all hung out in the weight room or the lap-swimming lanes.

The reminder sent Sailor's thoughts careening back to her lunchtime discussion—make that *arm-twisting*—with Kathy. She made a correction in her computer file, stabbed the EN-TER key, and flipped the third teacher's registration form face-down on the completed pile. "I cannot believe that girl."

Kathy, of course. Not the teacher. What had possessed her friend to think Sailor could possibly be coerced into joining the Bards of Birkenstock committee? She glared at the computer monitor. "I don't *do* committees—as if the whole universe doesn't know that already."

And yet. . .Kathy had let that one tempting morsel slip out. Chandler Michaels had been selected to receive the Birkenstock Arts and Letters Association's annual award for outstanding literary achievement. Every year they honored prominent Missouri authors at the Bards of Birkenstock Festival, an event that brought in Missouri's brightest literary luminaries for readings, book signings, a parade, and a $100-a-plate fund-raising dinner that culminated in the gala awards ceremony.

Chandler Michaels—right here in Birkenstock! And if Sailor joined the committee, she'd be guaranteed actual face time with the author who had set her heart aflutter with his heart-tugging love stories too many times to count.

An insistent buzzing nagged at her from somewhere beneath a pile of papers. She shuffled them aside until she exhumed her desk phone then jabbed the intercom button. "Hi, Gloria. What's up?"

"Phone call on line 3," the front-desk receptionist chirped. "It's your friend Kathy."

Expecting an answer, no doubt. "Thanks, Glo." She pressed another phone button and grabbed up the receiver. "I told you I needed some time to think about it."

"What's to think about? You're dying to meet Chandler Michaels. Admit it."

Sailor stretched her legs under the desk. "He's been away from Missouri so long, it would be just my luck he won't even come to town for the ceremony. You've seen the Oscars. The biggest stars are so busy with their next movie that they pre-tape their acceptance speeches and don't bother attending."

"Birkenstock's hometown hero? He'll come back if for no other reason than to gloat."

Sailor sat up straight, her breath quickening. "Chandler Michaels is from Birkenstock?"

"You didn't know? Since you love his books so much, I figured you'd know everything about the guy."

"I am *not* some crazed fan." Sailor winced. "Anyway, he's a very private person. His Web site bio just says he grew up in a small town in the Missouri Ozarks."

"Well, I just found out from our committee chairperson that Chandler was born and raised right here in little ol' Birky. His real name is Chuck Michalicek. 'Chandler Michaels' is his pen name." Kathy chuckled. "Can't say I blame him. Chuck Michalicek is quite a mouthful."

"Michalicek? The name's vaguely familiar. . . ." Sailor twisted the phone cord.

"I did a Web search myself. You're right—nothing linking Chandler Michaels to Birkenstock. But I dug up a mention of Chuck Michalicek on the Birky High Facebook page. The old guy graduated way before our time then apparently left for college and dropped off the local radar."

"*Old guy?* He can't be *that* old."

Kathy snorted. "I'm staring at his picture in a BHS yearbook as we speak. He looked way different then—mutton-chop sideburns, long-haired hippy 'do. 'Peace, brother' all the way."

Sailor cringed. "But he looks so handsome on his book covers."

"Surely you realize that publicity photo is a masterful work of airbrushing? And the dinner jacket, black tie, backlighting, the whole I'm-as-suave-as-James-Bond thing? Please."

"Well. . .it's a persona. Would you want to read a romance novel by an author who looked like Bill Gates?"

Kathy roared then quickly lowered her voice a notch. "If somebody as rich as Bill Gates wanted to romance me, I wouldn't care what he looked like."

Sailor looked up to see Gloria poking her strawberry blond head around the cubicle wall. The receptionist handed her another registration form and tapped a french-manicured fingernail on the printed name. "He's waiting out front right now—wants to ask some questions about your class."

He? Sailor's eyes widened then narrowed to slits. Probably an elderly retiree who found out the tai chi class was full. "I've got to go, Kathy," she said into the phone. "Can we talk about this later?"

"Just say yes. This is your chance, Sailor." Kathy mimicked a hyper game show host. "You, the one and only Sailor Kern, could be picking up Chandler Michaels from the airport. Driving Chandler Michaels around town. Arranging Chandler Michaels's autograph parties. Presenting Chandler Michaels with the Bards of Birkenstock commemorative plaque, engraved with his name—"

"Stop. Just stop!" Sailor grimaced and thrust out a hand. "Okay, I'll be on your stupid committee. Just promise I can stay in the background. No phone solicitations. No public speaking."

"We'll keep it very low-key, I promise. It'll be fun!"

Low-key, my toenail. Could there be *anything* low-key with Kathy? Sailor hung up the phone and wondered if she'd completely lost her sanity. Then a giggle erupted from deep in her belly and worked its way up through her chest until it exploded from her throat. She squeezed her eyes shut and pumped her fists.

"I'm going to meet Chandler Michaels!"

***

Parker paced the YMCA lobby, first peering through the steamy windows overlooking the indoor pool then pausing to watch the patrons using the health center. Swimming. Why couldn't Andy have suggested swimming? Wouldn't it stretch his back out as well as some wimpy water aerobics class?

"Hi. You wanted to see me?"

The tiny voice came from behind him, almost too soft to be heard over the clang and groan of the health-center weight machines. He glanced over his shoulder—stupid move, considering the jolt of pain it caused—and then had to drop his gaze nearly a foot to find the source of that voice.

"Hi. Are you the water aerobics instructor?" Couldn't be . . .could she? Five foot two if that, face devoid of makeup, dishwater blond hair pulled into a messy ponytail. She didn't even look old enough to have a driver's license.

"Sailor Kern. And you're Mr. . . . ." She scanned his registration form. "Parker?"

"Travis."

"Hi Travis, nice to meet you. What can I tell you about the class?"

"No, it's Parker. Parker Travis."

She crossed her arms and retreated a step. Eyes the color of the indoor pool shimmered under the fluorescent overheads. "Now I'm confused."

Perfect. He felt like he was in elementary school again. Except his teachers were never this youthful. Nor as unpretentiously pretty.

Yikes. *Get a grip, man.* "My name is Parker Travis, not Travis Parker."

Her gaze flitted across the form. "People are always missing that it says last name first and putting their first name first, so I thought. . ." Those aqua eyes gave an embarrassed roll and her tone grew even softer. "Well, anyway, Mr. *Travis*, Gloria said you had some questions."

"Yeah. My doctor recommended your class." Parker glanced around the lobby. A couple of jocks in gym shorts and sweaty T-shirts strolled out of the health center, their jibes and deep-throated laughter bouncing off the walls. Parker waited while the testosterone cloud dissipated. He could bench-press 200 pounds, and Andy wanted him to sign up for *water aerobics*?

"You were saying?"

Parker huffed a resigned sigh. "See, I've got this pain behind my right shoulder and the doc thought your class would help."

The girl shifted. A dubious gleam lit her narrowed eyes. "But you're not convinced."

Parker stared at the toes of his black sneakers. A dusting of gray hair clippings clung to them, reminding him of his conversation with the spunky ninety-year-old in the apartment next to Grams's. While he styled her hair today, he'd let it slip that he might be signing up for this class. She proudly flexed her rounded bicep, giving credit to her three-times-a-week water workouts with the "sweet little instructor" at the Y.

"Little" certainly described the pint-sized mass of lean muscle standing before him. He'd hold off on the "sweet" verdict for now. Striking a pose to mirror Miss Kern's, he said, "Let's just say I'm not sure if the class is right for me."

She shrugged. One eyebrow slowly lifted in what could only be interpreted as a challenge. "Only one way to find out."

Parker chewed his lip. He'd never live it down if he showed up for church Sunday and had to tell Andy he chickened out. "Okay, hit me with your best shot."

ૐ

Sailor tried to keep the delighted look off her face. Ever since her first glimpse of Parker Travis, she'd been fighting to keep her heartbeat steady. In nearly ten years of teaching at the Y, she'd had *maybe* that many male students, and most of them had been at least twice her age. She hadn't expected a halfway good-looking man in his midthirties *without* a weight problem and *with* a full head of hair. Parker was obviously physically fit, boyishly charming, good-looking in an understated sort of way. . . .

She double-checked the registration form.

Yes, and single!

Still in shock, she led her newest student through the double glass doors into the pool area. Immediately a deep sense of peace washed over her—the clear, ice blue water splish-splashing against the tiles, the moist heaviness in the chlorine-scented air, the broad windows overlooking the Y's forested jogging path. This place meant much more to her than merely a cavernous space housing an Olympic-size swimming pool. It had literally saved her life.

Parker Travis stepped up beside her. "Nice view."

"Isn't it?" Turning toward him, Sailor exhaled a calming breath.

His gaze swept the full length of her body before his mouth turned down in a doubtful grimace. "So do I need any special equipment?"

She shook off the shivery feeling his slow perusal had

evoked and drew herself up taller, not that it helped. "I usually e-mail the information to my students before the first class, but since you're here. . ." She strode across the deck, opened the door of a tall cabinet, and pulled out various pieces of gear. "You'll need a flotation belt, webbed gloves, aqua blocks, noodles—"

"Noodles? What are we going to do, make spaghetti?"

Laughter bubbled up from Sailor's abdomen. "A pool noodle is a five-foot length of compressed foam rubber. We use them for resistance or as a flotation aid." She retrieved a lime green noodle from the molded-plastic storage bin next to the cabinet. "The Y keeps all this gear on hand, but if you'd rather purchase your own, Sports and More carries a basic water aerobics kit. Just mention you're in my class, and they'll know what you want."

"Okay." Parker nodded thoughtfully. "Guess I'll see you tomorrow. Four o'clock, right?"

"Four o'clock."

Another crazy, tingly, girly feeling raced up her arms as she watched him leave. She recalled the logo on his shirt. Par Excellence Salon and Day Spa, that ritzy place just off downtown, where Birkenstock's beautiful people hung out to get even more beautiful. A memory clicked into place—wasn't Parker Travis the high school track star-turned hairstylist? Maybe she could garner some tips on how to look her best when Chandler Michaels arrived in town. Her reflection stared back at her from the tinted glass doors—a limp strand of stick-straight hair falling across one eye, knobby knees poking through faded sweatpants, a figure that was more soda straw than hourglass.

If she wanted to impress Chandler Michaels, she'd need all the help she could get.

two

Parker adjusted the folded towel behind Donna DuPont's neck and eased her head into the shampoo bowl. "Comfortable?"

"Perfectly. Use that luscious peach-scented stuff. I packed a bottle for our Maui vacation, and Howard went wild over it."

"Glad our illustrious mayor approved." Grinning, Parker turned on the sprayer to rinse out the Platinum Diva #39 he'd applied twenty minutes ago. "How was your trip?"

While the mayor's wife described luaus, dolphin watching, and snorkeling excursions, Parker nodded and set to work. No denying it, shampooing remained one of his favorite aspects of being a hairstylist. After wetting Donna's hair, he applied a generous dollop of Peaches 'n' Crème Ultra-Conditioning Shampoo and massaged it into frothy, fragrant suds. His fingers glided across Donna's lathered scalp in overlapping circles, the sensation as relaxing to him as it was to his sleepy-eyed client. *Let's see that water aerobics instructor top this for the ultimate in stress reduction.*

Great, just when he thought he'd put the dreaded class out of his mind. He checked his watch. *Hoo-boy.* The class started in less than an hour.

"Ouch!" Donna jerked beneath his fingers. "Good grief, Parker, you're not kneading bread dough."

"Sorry." He finished with a gentler massage and reached for the sprayer.

"You seem a tad distracted this afternoon," Donna said later as they returned to his station.

He rotated his shoulders a few times before removing her towel and beginning her comb-out. "Having some back trouble. I'm supposed to start an exercise class today."

"Ugh. Getting older is the pits." Donna turned her head from side to side. "Do you think I should go shorter?"

"Sure, we can do that." Parker squinted into the mirror. Was that a tinge of gray in his sideburns? *You're sure not getting any younger, Travis.* In only four years he'd hit the big 4-0. . .not that he was keeping track.

"Not Jamie Lee Curtis short, mind you. I need a little fullness around my face, don't you think?"

Parker shook off his depressing thoughts. "Now, Donna, have I ever let you walk out of here looking anything but gorgeous?"

"That's why I keep coming back." She giggled like a teeny-bopper. "You are quite a handsome man, you know."

The scissors slipped. Parker did a quick recovery and evened out the minor mishap before Donna could notice. He shot her an embarrassed smile through the mirror. "What would the mayor think if he knew you were flirting shamelessly with your hairdresser?"

"If I weren't already. . ." She tittered and dropped her volume. Not that it mattered with the constant chatter and the whir of blow-dryers emanating from the other cubicles. "What I mean is, any gal in town would have her socks knocked off to nab you for a husband. When are you going to find yourself a wife and settle down?"

He exhaled sharply and reached for the dryer. "Haven't met the right one, I guess."

"How do you expect to develop a lasting relationship, putting in the hours you do? And then donating your services at the assisted-living center, doing all those old ladies' hair?"

The ache in Parker's shoulder gave way to a bristle of irritation. "I love those sweet old gals."

Donna flicked a stray hair clipping off her nose. "Well, you ought to at least ask if any of them have a cute, available granddaughter—oops, at their age, better make it *great*-granddaughter."

❧

Seated on the poolside bleachers, Sailor looked from the registration forms to the aging "Doublemint Twins" bursting out of skirted fuchsia bathing suits. She'd been stunned to learn they really had starred in one of those Wrigley's gum commercials back in the '70s. "So. . .which one is Lucille and which one is Lorraine?"

"I'm Lucille."

"I'm Lorraine."

Sailor's breath whistled out. "My goodness, you *are* identical, aren't you?"

"It's easy to tell us apart once you get to know us." Lucille— or was it Lorraine?—cocked a plump hip and fluttered her sparse lashes. "I'm the cute one. My sister's the smart one."

Both burst out in gales of laughter. They pranced to the far end of the bleachers and began laying out their water aerobics gear.

Sailor groaned. This class could prove the most challenging mix of students yet. She turned her attention to the next arrivals, the three teacher friends from Birkenstock High. All reasonably fit, thank goodness, probably midfifties at most. Sailor checked them off her roster in time to welcome the new mom and the paralegal. She introduced them to the other ladies then peeked into the lobby. One more student expected, and he was already ten minutes late. Probably a no-show. Like she'd be surprised.

She let the glass door whisk shut then returned to the bleachers. Her students sat hip to hip on the first row, their expressions somewhere between eager and terrified. Maybe she should assure them she hadn't drawn and quartered anyone. . .yet. Offering a shy smile, she slid out of her sweatpants and adjusted the straps of her teal blue tank suit.

"Wel—" She cleared her throat of first-day jitters. "Welcome, everyone." She ought to be used to this by now. She always relaxed once the class got going, but those first moments facing a new group of strangers turned her insides to gelatin.

"Okay, let's get started." She collected her personal exercise equipment from the storage cabinet, along with extras for those who hadn't purchased their own. "Hop in the pool. I'll explain how to use everything once we're in the water."

With practiced ease she strode to the four-foot mark and stepped off, bouncing lightly as her toes hit bottom. The chilly water made her gasp.

The Doublemint Twins—she *must* get their names straight—tested the water with fuchsia-painted toenails.

"Oooh, that's cold!" Lorraine—or was it Lucille?—shivered and hugged herself.

"Once we get moving, it won't be so bad." Sailor motioned to the ladder. "You can ease in more gradually if you'd rather."

While the twins made their way down the ladder, huffing and complaining all the way, the other ladies put their legs over the edge and splashed themselves before sliding into the pool. Sailor began by showing them how to hold their noodles at arm's length, moving them forward and back just below the surface as they marched in place.

The door from the lobby burst open. The guy from yesterday careened around the end of the bleachers. What was his name? Travis Parker, Parker Travis, whatever. "Sorry I'm late."

Sailor pursed her lips and kept marching. Good-looking and single he might be, but she despised having her class interrupted. "It's"—*inhale*—"okay"—*exhale*. "Please get a noodle and join us. We're beginning with warm-ups and stretches."

"Noodle. Yeah, the long foam thingy." He grabbed one and tossed it into the pool then kicked black sneakers off sockless feet, tore a white T-shirt over his head, and splashed into the water next to the paralegal. "Hi. I'm Parker Travis."

"Oh, the Par Excellence stylist! I just moved to Birkenstock, and I've been meaning to make an appointment. Everyone says you're the best in town." The paralegal released one end of her noodle and stuck out her hand. "Miranda Wright."

Sailor choked on a chuckle and covered it with a cough. Seeing the name on a registration form was one thing, but hearing it aloud was even funnier. Did Miranda's parents have any clue she'd end up in a law profession?

Sailor composed herself and raised her voice. "*Quiet* warm-ups and stretching, everyone. Please save your social time for after class."

"Sorry, my bad." The hairdresser. And wearing cutoff jeans, of all things. Goose bumps rose on his pale chest beneath a tanned V that suggested he spent time outdoors in a T-shirt. A runner—of course. His muscled limbs bore the telltale look of someone who worked out but didn't take stretches seriously. No wonder his doctor had recommended Sailor's class.

Sailor slanted him an annoyed frown. "Are you aware the Y has a no-cutoffs policy?"

He apologized again. "My old suit was worn-out. Didn't think you'd appreciate the, uh, view."

With effort Sailor kept her cool through the rest of the class, despite the twins' giggling and the hairdresser's grunts and groans as they attempted various exercises.

Chandler Michaels. Chandler Michaels. Chandler Michaels.

That name would sustain her for the duration of this class. The third weekend in May and the Bards of Birkenstock Festival could not come soon enough.

&

The water aerobics class could not end soon enough. Parker only thought he'd kept himself fit. He hadn't felt this hammered down, twisted up, and bent out of shape since third grade, when he wrapped his bicycle—and himself—around a sycamore sapling. And Andy said this would be good for his back pain? He'd be lucky if he could pry himself out of bed tomorrow morning, let alone make it through a day at the salon. Hard to believe Grams and her friends actually did this stuff several times a week—and claimed to enjoy it.

The last to trudge up the pool steps, Parker stowed his exercise equipment in the cabinet. He limped up beside Sailor as she answered some questions from those plump, giggly twins with the bad perms.

"It gets easier, right?" one of the twins asked.

"Of course." Sailor handed each woman a sheet of paper. "Here's your practice routine. Try to work in at least two or three sessions before next time, and—"

Parker eased his cramping left thigh. "You mean we're supposed to do this on our own, too?"

Sailor nailed him with her aquamarine stare. "You can't expect to reap the benefits if you only work out once a week."

"I get that, but—" Parker sucked air between his teeth. Man, one hour with this skinny little water aerobics teacher and he felt like a bumbling oaf.

One of the twins released a chirpy laugh. "Honey, if two old biddies like us can do this, you sure can. Let's go shower, Lucille. We can have the early bird special at Audra's Café and still be home in time for *Wheel of Fortune*."

The twins gave him an eyeful of their fuchsia-clad rumps as they waddled toward the ladies' dressing room. He should have given them his card and offered to do something about those horrible perms.

Sailor's shoulders lifted in an exaggerated sigh. She pressed one of the practice sheets into his hand. "You'll get it. Just. . .try not to be late next time. And get some trunks."

"Guess I didn't make a very good first impression on the teacher." He stared at the page, a series of photographs with brief descriptions. Jogging in place. Arm extensions. Side-to-side lunges. Maybe Grams could give him some pointers.

"Don't be so hard on yourself. This was only your first class." With the grace of a ballerina, Sailor glided across the deck and bent from the waist to gather up her gear.

Parker found himself staring at the sleek curve of her profile, the muscle definition in those skinny arms, the wet tangle of her ponytail curling across one shoulder.

Whoa, fella! He gave himself a mental shake. Donna Du-Pont had done a fine job of reminding him he was *way* over the hill already. This little thing was probably fresh out of high school, if that. There were laws.

She carried her gear to the storage cabinet then looked his way in surprise. "Did you have more questions?"

Parker rubbed his chin. "I, uh. . ."

"I'd be happy to talk more on the way out, but I have another commitment this evening."

"Don't let me hold you up." Parker slid into his shoes and edged toward the door. "Same time next week?"

"Every Tuesday at four o'clock." She gave an exhausted moan. "For seven more weeks."

࿐

"Seven more weeks of the Douglas twins?" Kathy draped an arm around Sailor's shoulders. "I've been putting up with their screechy voices in church choir for two years now. Oh, how I pity you!"

"Douglas, Doublemint. Lorraine, Lucille. I never did get their names right." Sailor sank into one of the empty chairs around the massive table in the library conference room. "So are we early or what?"

"The rest of the committee usually drags in by ten after seven." Kathy began distributing notepads and pens around the table. "And Donna DuPont, the chair, just got back from vacationing in Hawaii, so she's probably still on aloha time."

"Hawaii. Sounds wonderful." Sailor slid deeper into the padded seat and folded her hands across her purple sweater. "Someday I'm going to take a vacation. A real one."

"You're already a world traveler. India, Guyana, Kenya. . . The farthest I've been outside Birkenstock is the librarians' convention in San Diego last year."

"Visiting my missionary parents every few years doesn't exactly constitute a vacation." Sailor's gaze settled upon an easel displaying a poster-size print of Chandler Michaels's latest book cover. Her heart faltered. "When I'm Mrs. Chandler Michaels, I'll invite you to my vacation villa on the Riviera. You can stay as long as you like."

Coming around the table, Kathy whacked her on the head with a notepad. "When are you going to pull your nose out of those romance novels and get serious about a real guy? Besides, how do you know Chandler isn't married with ten kids?"

"His bio says he lives in a New York apartment with his Siamese cat. No mention of a wife or kids."

"But if he keeps his private life private. . ."

"I'm reading between the lines." _And hoping._ Maybe it was a silly schoolgirl fantasy, but she couldn't stop herself from dreaming.

Two more committee members drifted in, and Sailor pulled herself erect. A twinge of nerves churned the remains of the tofu stir-fry she'd made for her and Uncle Ed's supper. Poor guy, she'd turn him into a healthy eater if it took the rest of his life.

"Hello, I don't believe we've met." An elderly gentleman with a shock of white hair took the chair next to hers. The mixed aromas of coffee and wintergreen tickled her nose. "Allan Biltmore, at your service."

Oh yes, the retired English teacher. Sailor had missed his class by one year. "Sailor Kern. I'm Kathy's friend." Except right now she wanted to strangle Kathy. How had she ever let her friend talk her into joining the Bards of Birkenstock committee?

Ba-ding. Chandler Michaels, that's how.

A few more committee members arrived, taking seats around the table. They took turns introducing themselves, but Sailor knew she'd never keep them all straight. Her brain felt like a washing machine on spin cycle, and the meeting hadn't even started yet.

As Kathy predicted, Donna DuPont didn't grace them with

her presence until nearly seven thirty. The platinum blond mayor's wife breezed to the head of the table, a Hawaiian-print muumuu swirling around her hips. "Sorry, sorry, sorry to keep you all waiting. I see Kathy's been playing hostess. Thanks for getting the room ready, dear."

Kathy nudged Sailor's chair and slipped her a Cheshire cat smile. "My pleasure, Donna. How was Hawaii?"

"Marvelous!" She took her seat then spent the next ten minutes describing the sights, smells, and sounds of Maui, until Allan Biltmore interrupted her with a loud *ahem* and suggested they get on with the meeting.

At least with everyone else present, Sailor could blend into the background. She tuned out the conversation and doodled on her notepad until Donna announced the next item on the agenda: Chandler Michaels's arrival in Birkenstock.

"It's confirmed, ladies and gentlemen, and I am *so* excited." Donna stood, as if to give her next words even more import. "Chandler will be flying in on the Tuesday before the festival, so we'll have him in town for five glorious days!"

Applause and cheers sounded around the table. Goose bumps traveled Sailor's limbs beneath her sweater and jeans.

"Some of you already know that Chandler is actually Birkenstock's own Charles Michalicek." Donna paused for a couple of surprised gasps. "Yes, it's true. And he's so excited for the chance to visit his hometown again. However, his family no longer lives in the area, so Allan has graciously offered to host Chandler in his home, which will save the committee some hotel expenses."

More applause and nods of approval. "And now I'll turn this portion of the discussion over to Kathy Richmond, who is heading up the Chandler Michaels welcome-committee task force." Donna extended her hand toward Kathy and sat down.

Kathy gave Sailor a quick wink as she scooted closer to the table. "Actually, the task force is just two of us at this point. My friend Sailor here is a huge fan of Chandler's, so she's agreed to help coordinate his schedule while he's in town."

Heat slithered up Sailor's neck. She could feel everyone's gaze shifting in her direction. Arms crossed over her midsection, she eased her chair backward a quarter inch and kept her eyes lowered.

Kathy flipped through a folder of notes. "I'm still waiting for a return phone call from Chandler's assistant, a Mr. Easley, but I assume he'll want as much PR exposure as possible." She itemized preliminary ideas for Chandler's visit—book signings, dinners, tickets to see his favorite Branson entertainer, the festival parade through downtown Birkenstock.

"Wonderful ideas, Kathy. It sounds like you have it all under control. And welcome to our committee, Sailor." Donna checked off another item on her agenda. "That about wraps up our business for tonight. Do I hear a motion to adjourn?"

❧

Sailor slumped into the living room and sagged against the back of Uncle Ed's recliner. While teaching a water aerobics class usually energized her—at least until today's group showed up—meetings of any kind drained the life out of her.

"Late night, eh?" Uncle Ed slid a bookmark into his John Adams biography and laid the book on the end table. "Your parents called."

Disappointment blanketed Sailor's shoulders. She and her parents e-mailed regularly, but with their crazy schedules and the time difference, she hadn't talked to them in over a month. She trudged to the sofa and sank down. "Rats. Sorry I missed them. How are they?"

"Your dad's knee-deep in another Bible translation, and your mom is heading out to the wilds tomorrow to set up a health clinic." He clucked his tongue. "Why they want to burn themselves out trying to save folks in some third-world country is beyond me."

"They're not burning themselves out, Uncle Ed. They're serving God."

"Like I said, burning themselves out." A look of loneliness darkened his eyes. He sighed and reached for his book.

Sailor shook her head. Poor Uncle Ed hadn't been the same since Aunt Trina died of a heart attack eighteen years ago, the day after Christmas the year Sailor turned fifteen. Uncle Ed blamed Aunt Trina's death on the stress of cooking for the 172 needy and homeless folks who signed up for the Mission Hills Bible Church Christmas dinner. He never went to church again, and his mental state began a slow but steady decline. Staying with her uncle might not be the greatest thing for her already limited social life, but Sailor didn't have the heart to leave him to fend for himself.

The mantel clock chimed nine forty-five. Sailor heaved herself off the sofa. "I'm heading to bed. Good night, Uncle Ed." She patted his shoulder, but his only response was a grunt.

Without turning on the light, she sank onto the edge of her bed. Truth be told, she wasn't all that much closer to God than her uncle. She still believed, but God seemed even farther away than her missionary parents in that tiny Kenyan settlement.

When had it started, this sense of aloneness? Probably the year she entered second grade and her parents decided to leave her in the States. Already past forty when Sailor was born, Ogden and Hazel Kern weren't exactly kid people anyway. They'd hoped she'd have a better life with Uncle Ed and Aunt Trina, who desperately wanted children but had none of their own.

Then Aunt Trina died. Sailor's parents arranged a hasty three-month furlough but then returned to the field, leaving Sailor to manage a grieving man's household while surviving high school. Without the guidance of church friends Josh and Deb Fanning—almost like second parents—she might not have made it. As Uncle Ed retreated into his biographies and woodworking, Sailor found solace in romance novels and comfort food. She must have put on seventy pounds between her freshman year and graduation. Her parents, returning home for the big event after nearly three years of seeing their daughter only in photographs, hardly recognized her.

Framed by the light from the hallway, Sailor glimpsed her dim reflection in the dresser mirror—a shadow of her former self, literally. It took a brush with borderline diabetes in college before she got serious about losing weight. Her doctor's threats, combined with encouragement from Josh and Deb, turned her onto healthy eating and exercise. She slimmed down, shaped up, and before she knew it, the Y had promoted her from part-time receptionist to water aerobics and swimming instructor.

But even after dropping sixty-five pounds and getting into the best shape of her life, Sailor still had trouble thinking of herself as pretty. Plain, boring Sailor Kern, the missionaries' kid. Whatever possessed her to imagine she could turn the head of someone like Chandler Michaels?

three

The following Tuesday Parker met his grandmother in the assisted-living center's small two-station salon. She beamed up at him from her motorized wheelchair. "Thanks for making a special trip. Yesterday was the only day Dr. Mendoza could work me in for my checkup." She fluffed her white curls and studied her reflection. "Do you think it's time for another perm yet?"

Parker tugged on a soft, silvery lock. "Couple more weeks maybe. You've still got a lot of body."

Grams chuckled. "You're the expert. I do think it's getting a bit long around the ears, though."

"Let's get you shampooed, and I'll have you trimmed up in no time." Parker helped her to the shampoo bowl.

Finishing up, he reached for a dry towel on the shelf above the sink. Pain arced across his shoulder blades. "Yow!"

"Parker, are you all right?" Grams sat forward, her old bones creaking.

"Just a cramp." Parker shook off the twinge before he worried his grandmother any further. Suffering from rheumatoid arthritis, she had enough problems of her own.

"Just a cramp indeed." Grams gripped the arms of the chair and skewered Parker with her steely blue gaze. "You've been moaning about your sore back for weeks. Isn't the water aerobics helping?"

"Hard to tell yet. I've only had one class." Parker helped Grams across the small space to the styling chair then patted her hair with the towel. He tried not to let the pain show in his face, but one glimpse in the mirror and he knew he couldn't fool anyone.

Grams absently massaged the gnarled knuckles of one hand. "I can't even imagine how much worse off I'd be if not for that sweet little instructor. I've been taking her classes for five years now, and she's always so patient and understanding."

Parker stifled a grimace as he combed up sections of his grandmother's wet curls and reshaped her style with precision snips. Sweet little instructor, huh? How about a ninety-five-pound Ivan the Terrible? The petite Miss Kern would not be pleased to know he'd opted to run and do weights rather than practice his pool exercises.

He flicked on the blow-dryer and coaxed strands of Grams's hair around a ceramic styling brush. The slick, soothing feel of each curl beneath his fingers drew his thoughts away from the ever-present ache between his shoulder blades. As he worked, a snippet of Grams's earlier remarks resurfaced. He paused and switched off the dryer. "She's been teaching five years already? What'd she do, start in kindergarten?"

Grams shot him a puzzled glance through the mirror. "Don't be silly. She has a college degree in exercise therapy from Missouri State."

He was now officially impressed. He sectioned off a lock of hair and wrapped it around the brush. "Well, she doesn't look a day over sixteen. That's all I can say."

❧

"Sailor Kern, you disgust me." Kathy drizzled ketchup on the mound of french fries next to her double-deluxe bacon burger. "You never let a gram of saturated fat slip past your lips, you're skinny as a model, and you don't look like you've aged a day since college."

Sailor flaked off a bite of broiled salmon topping her Asian salad, one of her favorites when she met Kathy for lunch at Audra's Café. "You know very well what I looked like my first year at MO State. Some days I'd kill for a greasy burger. But I love being healthy too much to risk it."

"What—eating the burger or getting nailed for murder?"

Laughing, Sailor flicked a spinach leaf across the table. "One of these days I'll convince you to try my class. I've incorporated a nutrition segment into my continuing series."

"No thank you. In the official Kathy Richmond dictionary, *nutrition* is a four-letter word." Kathy dabbed a dribble of hamburger juice off her chin. "Psyched for another class with the Douglas twins?"

Sailor slumped. "Why'd you have to remind me?"

"A slice of Audra's homemade turtle cheesecake would sure help ease the pain." Kathy signaled their server. "Want me to order one for you?"

"I'm almost desperate enough to be tempted, but. . ." Sailor sat back and patted her abdomen. "Two words: *Chandler Michaels.*"

"Puleeeze, you are not still harboring romantic notions about the guy?"

When Sailor didn't answer right away, Kathy made a growling noise and hammered the table with her fists. "Sailor, honey, Chandler Michaels is a fantasy. Find yourself a nice, stable, hometown guy. Somebody who's proud enough of his Birkenstock roots not to run off to the big city and change his name."

Sailor's chest tightened. "I'm thirty-two years old, and I have yet to meet one eligible guy who'd even look at me twice."

"Come on, Sailor. . ."

"No, it's true." An image of the raven-haired beauty gracing the cover of Chandler's latest novel filled her mind. She whispered a sigh and stared at a soggy lettuce leaf at the bottom of her salad plate. "Maybe you should get someone else for the committee. I don't think I'm the right person after all."

Kathy poked Sailor's arm with the tines of her fork. "You stop talking like that right now. There's no one I'd rather have working with me."

"I know, but—"

"I know how much you admire Chandler. But it kills me to see you mooning over an aging literary snob, when I'm certain God has someone really, really special in mind for you."

Sailor huffed. "Well, He's sure taking His own sweet time." Her shoulders relaxed, and a shy grin crept across her face. "But I admit, I've let myself get a little too starry-eyed over the idea of meeting Chandler."

"He will be one lucky guy having you squire him around town." Kathy finished off the last of her burger. "And if he turns out to be totally cool and even a tenth as charming as his story heroes, I'll be incredibly jealous."

Audra, the café owner, arrived at their booth to personally deliver Kathy's turtle cheesecake. "I heard Chandler Michaels is coming to town for the book festival." She flipped her auburn pageboy off her shoulder. "Back when he was just plain 'Chuck,' he gave me my first kiss. Any chance you can wrangle me a date with him?"

Kathy shrank back, one hand to her chest. "Why, Audra, aren't you and Hank celebrating an anniversary soon?"

"Number twenty-seven." Audra tipped her head back and laughed. "But I'm dying to see how the years have changed Chuck. I've already scheduled my hair appointment at Par Excellence for that week. Gotta look my best for the gala. I'm catering, you know."

Sailor fingered the end of her ponytail. Par Excellence— the logo on her new student's shirt. "Audra, do you know the guy who works there—Travis something?"

"Parker Travis. He's the *best*." She smoothed the curve of her pageboy. "Wouldn't let anyone else lay a hand on these tresses."

Kathy nudged Sailor's ankle with her toe. "How do you know Parker?"

"He's in my water aerobics class that just started."

"*He's* the weirdo guy you were telling me about—the one who showed up late and then griped for the entire hour?" Kathy guffawed. "Why didn't you tell me?"

"Can I help it I have a problem with names?" Sailor crossed her arms. "So what's the big deal?"

Kathy shared a look with Audra. "Good grief, Sailor. Parker

Travis is probably *the* most eligible bachelor in Birkenstock."

Audra scooted onto the seat next to Kathy and clicked her enameled fake nails on the tabletop. "Not to mention he's one marvelous hairstylist."

"Well, he's a lousy student." Sailor looped her arm through the strap of her tan microfiber ergonomic purse and edged out of the booth. "I'll let you two dish the hairdresser. I've got to get back to the Y."

ঙ

In the Willow Tree parking lot, Parker dropped his styling kit onto the backseat of his Camry then collapsed behind the wheel and gave his shoulder a rub before starting the engine. Just enough time to run home and change into his new swim trunks before heading to the Y.

That was the plan anyway. Now, as he stood before his closet mirror, he took one look at himself in the psychedelic orange fabric and decided to risk Miss Kern's ire one more week with his faded cutoffs. After he explained the local department store was a little late stocking its spring line of bathing suits and was still selling off last year's leftovers, maybe she'd cut him some slack.

The pool area stood empty except for the lifeguard and two guys doing the backstroke in the lap lanes. Sailor Kern was nowhere in sight. He gathered a set of exercise gear from the tall cabinet and chose a bright yellow noodle from the storage bin. In the water he turned toward the windows overlooking the jogging trail and tried a few stretching and warm-up exercises. At least now he could truthfully say he'd practiced.

Between the hushed water sounds and the pleasant view, Parker found his shoulders relaxing into the stretches. His breathing deepened. His heart rate steadied.

"Nice. Very nice."

Parker jerked his head around. The voice may have been gentle, but the effect on his psyche—and his achy shoulders— was anything but. He shifted to face his petite instructor. "Just warming up."

"So I see." Holding an aqua blue noodle, Sailor descended into the pool as softly as a feather on a spring breeze. Arms draped across the noodle, she drew her knees up and frowned. "Didn't I mention the Y's policy about cutoffs?"

Parker wiggled an eyebrow. "If you saw the only trunks Mabry's had in my size, you'd be thanking me for wearing the cutoffs."

The corner of her mouth turned up in the beginnings of a smile, but she quickly looked away. Embarrassed? Shy? Funny how she masterfully took control of a class of complaining adults, yet every other time he saw her, she conveyed a bashful vulnerability. Confident one moment, timid the next. . . He found it hard to believe she wasn't as youthful as she appeared.

Maybe the perennial haze shrouding the pool had something to do with it. The misty air would certainly mask a crow's-foot or two. But when he signed up for the class last week, he'd seen her in the full, harsh glow of the lobby lights. Nope, not a wrinkle or crow's-foot in sight.

He stretched his legs behind him and draped his arms over the noodle. "I heard you've been teaching classes here for several years."

"Close to ten, I guess." That shy smile again.

Parker tried to keep his face expressionless while he did the mental arithmetic. Eighteen when she finished high school, at least twenty-two out of college, then another ten years teaching for the Y. So. . .thirty-something?

No way! An enigma. Sailor Kern was definitely an enigma.

She stretched from side to side with the elegance of a water nymph. He attempted a few nonchalant lunges with the grace of a hippopotamus.

Her barely disguised smirk did nothing for his ego. "How's your back this week? Any improvement?"

He gave a noncommittal grunt.

"It'll come. Here, try this." She showed him how to adjust his stance to increase the stretch.

He felt the release in his tender back muscle and huffed out a long, slow breath. "Wow, that helped. I do the ladies' hair over at Willow Tree Assisted-Living Center. They all rave about you, in case you didn't know it."

Sailor's face brightened. "I really look forward to those classes."

As opposed to this one, judging from the wistful look in her eyes. She checked her watch then shifted a nervous glance toward the door.

He was about to ask how she got started teaching water aerobics when giggles and high-pitched voices announced the arrival of the Douglas twins. Sailor hoisted herself out of the pool to greet them, the phoniest smile he'd ever seen plastered across her face. After last week he felt pretty certain she couldn't be *that* glad to see the noisy duo. Nope, he suspected this was all about avoiding further conversation with him.

Within a few minutes the other students filtered in, and by the time everyone got situated in the water, Sailor had her confident instructor persona firmly in place. She hardly glanced in Parker's direction for the duration of the class.

And he couldn't take his eyes off her.

&

Sailor stuffed the last neon-colored noodle into the storage bin and slammed the lid shut. Though Parker Travis and the rest of her class had left ten minutes ago, she could still feel the sinewy hairstylist's penetrating stare. Time for a long, hard lap swim.

After eight laps of churning up the water with her freestyle, she switched to breaststroke, stretching her limbs and enjoying the easy glide. When she reached the wall at the deep end, she looked up to see her friend Josh Fanning, the silver-haired swim-team coach, grinning down at her.

"Too bad you're not in high school anymore. We could sure use you on the team."

"In high school you wouldn't have wanted me on the team." In one smooth move Sailor pushed out of the water and onto the deck. She scraped both palms along her slicked-back hair and wrung out her ponytail, water droplets cascading across her shoulders. "Remember when you first gave me swimming lessons? I could barely make it half a length without choking."

"Ah yes. Fishing you out of the pool, drying your tears—"

"Throwing me back in, making me swim another lap." Sailor smirked. "If you hadn't stayed on my case about exercise, plus Deb's insistence on healthy eating, I hate to think where I'd be today."

"How many times do I have to tell you? Deb and I love you like one of our own kids." Josh knelt to dip his goggles in the pool then tugged them on and pressed them into his eye sockets. He stepped off the edge and plunged deep before bobbing to the surface and treading water. "Almost forgot. Deb told me to invite you over for dinner one night this week. When's good for you?"

"Any night but tonight. I've got a"—Sailor cringed—"a meeting."

"A meeting? You?" Josh moved his goggles up to his forehead and squinted at her. "Can't be anything at the Y, or I'd know about it. What have you gotten yourself into, young lady?"

"Promise you won't laugh?" She dangled her feet in the water while she told him about the Bards of Birkenstock committee and Chandler Michaels's expected arrival. "I had no idea he grew up here. His real name is Chuck. . .Chuck. . .something Eastern European, I think."

"Not Chuck Michalicek?"

"That's it. Did you know him?"

"Oh yeah." Josh hooked one tanned arm over the coping. A funny smile quirked his lips. "So ol' Chuck Michalicek is coming back to Birkenstock. He was a couple years behind me in school. Biggest cutup on the swim team. Late for practice, smoked in the locker room. Loved playing practical jokes, especially on the girls." Josh chuckled. "Had us guys convinced he'd hidden a camera in the girls' dressing room. After two weeks of the girls complaining and the guys begging Chuck to show him the pictures, he finally admitted it was a hoax."

Sailor ignored the prickles climbing up her spine. "I'm sure he's matured since then."

"One can only hope." Josh settled his goggles into place again and pushed off the wall in a powerful butterfly stroke.

Sailor watched in admiration for a few minutes before grabbing her towel and heading to the dressing room. Clad in jeans and a forest green pullover, she returned to her desk and retrieved her purse from the bottom drawer. Beneath it she found the copy of *Love's Sweet Song*. She turned it over and gazed at the photo of Chandler Michaels. If a trace remained of the "bad boy" Josh had described, she couldn't see it. . .unless it shone in that mischievous sparkle behind his enticing baby blues.

Man, he was handsome! Sailor's heart did a deep *ker-thump* that made her catch her breath. So what if he was several years older? What she wouldn't give to have Chandler Michaels turn those dreamy eyes her way!

And the likelihood of that? Slim to none. Sailor flicked the end of her damp ponytail off her shoulder. Looking like a drowned rat sure didn't increase her odds. She sank onto her steno chair, her hopes evaporating once again.

Then her glance fell upon the water aerobics class roster, and the name *Parker Travis* jumped out at her. Everyone claimed he was the best hairstylist in town. Maybe it was time she scheduled an appointment.

four

"Mmm, smells good." Parker planted a hello kiss on his mother's cheek before lifting the lid off the slow cooker. When Mom phoned yesterday with a last-minute plea for his flute-playing talents then bribed him with an early lunch of his favorite beef Stroganoff, how could he refuse? Fortunately his Saturday-afternoon clients were willing to reschedule or see one of the other stylists.

His mother slapped his hand. "Careful, you're letting the heat out."

"Picky, picky." He let the glass lid drop into place. "Can I do anything?"

"You can see if Grams has any last-minute tips. She's in the den, watching the video of last Saturday's show."

"I can't believe I let you talk me into this." A part-time dental hygienist, Mom also sang backup for Frankie Verona on weekends at the legendary jazz singer's Branson theater. Parker had been invited to jam with Frankie's band a few times when he'd gone down to watch his mom at rehearsals, so when Frankie's regular flutist came down with the stomach flu following last night's show, Mom had volunteered Parker as a convenient substitute for the Saturday matinee and evening performances.

She set a salad bowl on the counter and unscrewed the cap from a bottle of Caesar dressing. "What's this your grandmother tells me about your taking water aerobics?"

"Guess I forgot to mention it." Parker plucked at a strand of his mother's chestnut hair. "Your roots are showing. Want to come in next week for a touch-up?"

"Can't. I traded my day off with Missy. She has another prenatal appointment." His mother carried the salad bowl to the table. "And changing the subject will not get me off your case. Why didn't you tell me about the exercise class?"

Parker sank onto a chair. "I just. . .feel kind of weird about it."

"Because water aerobics is not—*ahem*—macho?" His mother fussed with a plaid placemat. "So you're no Marc Bulger. You don't have to play pro football for the St. Louis Rams to be considered manly."

He looked askance toward the coatrack by the back door. A dry cleaner's bag covered the black leather jeans and silver satin shirt his mother had borrowed from the ailing flutist, who—also conveniently—was close to Parker in size. "Dressing like a magician's assistant doesn't exactly help."

"Parker Travis, when have you ever cared what other people thought?"

He combed his fingers through his hair. When *had* he started caring how others perceived his masculinity? Certainly not in high school as the only male flutist in the marching band. He got teased plenty back then, but it rolled off his back like shampoo suds sliding down the drain. Manliness, in his mind, had more to do with strength of character, integrity, honoring your responsibilities. Secure in his identity as a child of God, he'd scoffed at his detractors and went on to pursue the career he felt called to.

True, there were those in the church who liked to quote Proverbs 31:30 to him, especially the line, "Charm is deceptive, and beauty is fleeting." Or the passage in 1 Peter addressed to women: "Your beauty should not come from outward adornment, such as braided hair and the wearing of gold jewelry and fine clothes. Instead, it should be that of your inner self, the unfading beauty of a gentle and quiet spirit, which is of great worth in God's sight."

Personally Parker took great joy in helping a woman's outer beauty reflect the beauty he saw inside, and he'd always had the sense that God approved. The Lord sure didn't skimp on beauty in scripture—beauty for ashes, the beautiful feet of the messenger upon the mountain, the beauty of Queen Esther, Jerusalem's Beautiful Gate. . . .

The soft hum of a motor preceded Grams's entrance. One of the most beautiful women in Parker's life, she coasted her motorized wheelchair to a stop next to his elbow. Gnarled fingers reached up to pat his arm. "What's got my boy looking so glum? Did that sweet little gal from the Y turn you down?"

"Sweet little gal?" Parker's mom plopped a stack of plates on the table and skewered him with her stare. "What else haven't you told me?"

Parker angled his grandmother a warning glance. "Nothing. Really."

Grams shot him a feisty look of her own. "Parker Travis, how do you ever expect to find the right girl if you refuse to ask anyone out?"

Mom turned to Grams. "Who is it? Someone from his exercise class?"

"The instructor." Grams nodded. "The same young lady my Willow Tree friends and I take from."

"Sailor Kern?" His mother's eyes lit up. "Why, Parker—"

"Mom!" He rose and marched to the other side of the table. Anything to put space between him and his meddling, matchmaking matrons.

His grinning mother planted her knuckles on the table and leaned toward him. "What's keeping you from asking her out? She's such a nice girl."

Mom would only scoff if he confessed how inept he felt in the romance department. Donna DuPont was right—between his salon work, volunteering, and making sure he was around whenever Mom or Grams needed anything, he'd kept himself too busy to even think about a relationship.

He crossed his arms. "She's nice, all right, if you go for the drill-sergeant type."

"That little bit of a thing? She's one of Dr. Simpson's patients. I've cleaned her teeth a few times, and she's as sweet as can be. And so pretty, too. I've always admired her eyes, the color of polished turquoise."

Just listening to his mother describe Sailor made his insides go all mushy. He circled the table and grabbed the water glasses Mom had left sitting on the counter. "Let's eat. We don't want to be late for the preshow rehearsal."

&

"Dibs on the remote."

"No fair! I had it first."

"Hey, it's my turn. I was going to play my new video game."

Laughing at the squabbling Fanning boys, Sailor ducked in time to avoid a badly tossed sofa pillow. Whenever Josh and Deb's five sons were all home at once, the place became a madhouse. Sailor didn't mind, though. This was one crowd scene that didn't make her want to hide under her bed.

"Boys!" Deb stood in the kitchen doorway, carrot-colored curls framing her warning glare. "You break your dad's new HDTV, and you'll be mowing lawns for the next ten years."

The "boys"—a brawny high schooler, three handsome college men, and a newlywed barely back from his honeymoon—turned to their mother with a collective groan. Tom, the newlywed, made an exaggerated display of fluffing the pillow and placing it just so on the sofa. Under his breath he muttered, "Party pooper."

Deb merely rolled her eyes and motioned Sailor out of the line of fire. "Come keep us girls company in the kitchen. I need your opinion on a new quinoa recipe."

"I love that stuff—so versatile." Sailor dodged number two son Ken's feigned bout of stomach upset. The boys didn't share their mother's penchant for health food.

In the kitchen Sailor joined Jeannie, Tom's perky bride, at the breakfast bar, where Deb had set out forks next to a savory sampling of curried quinoa.

Sailor tasted a bite and grinned her appreciation. "Yum. Make sure you give me the recipe."

Jeannie sampled a forkful, but the look on her pixie-shaped

face suggested the dish wasn't exactly the most delicious thing she'd ever tasted. "Interesting mix of flavors."

"It's an acquired taste, but really healthy." Sailor helped herself to another bite. "How long are you and Tom in town, Jeannie?"

"Just for the weekend." Jeannie popped the top on a diet soda. "We both have to be back at work in KC on Monday morning."

The low rumble of the garage door sent a vibration through the floor beneath Sailor's feet. Seconds later Josh stepped into the kitchen. "Hello, ladies." He buzzed a kiss across Deb's lips before whipping an envelope from his back pocket. "Guess what I have in my hot little hands."

Deb fingered her chin. "The deed to our own private island in the Caribbean? The title to a new Mercedes?"

Josh snickered as he made a show of lifting the envelope flap. "Nope, what I have here is our evening's entertainment— four tickets to the Frankie Verona show tonight in Branson."

"Be still, my heart!" Deb faked a swoon and landed in Josh's arms.

Jeannie arched an eyebrow. "Who's Frankie Verona?"

"You've never heard of Frankie Verona, jazz singer extraordinaire?" Sailor glanced around the kitchen in search of one of the CD cases Deb usually left lying around. She spotted one on the verdigris baker's rack and handed it to Jeannie. "Frankie's 'Moonlight over Missouri' is Josh and Deb's favorite song."

Deb started humming the tune, and Josh swept her into an impromptu waltz around the kitchen. "I can't believe it," Deb said. "We're seeing Frankie tonight? How'd you manage that?"

"A gift from an anonymous Y patron, that's all I know. I found the envelope on my desk after my swim classes." Josh lowered Deb into a dip. "Eight o'clock show, front-row seats. Now we just have to decide who gets to go with us."

"Go where?" Tom ambled into the kitchen. "And what's with the *Dancing with the Stars* routine?"

Sailor finished off the sample plate of curried quinoa and licked her lips. "Your dad got tickets to the Frankie Verona show. You and Jeannie should go with them." She'd keep it to herself that the tickets had actually been left for her. A courier had delivered them to the Y around eleven that morning but refused to reveal the benefactor. Sailor guessed it had to be one of her students, but knowing how much Josh and Deb loved Frankie, she decided they'd enjoy the tickets even more than she.

Jeannie snuggled under her husband's arm and stole a kiss. "Sounds like fun, but tonight's my friend's baby shower, remember? That's why Tom and I are in town."

"Oh, right." Deb disentangled herself from Josh's embrace. "Then who can we share the other two tickets with?"

Tom swiped a swig of Jeannie's diet soda. "You can still take me. I'm sure not going to any ol' baby shower."

"Great, but that leaves one more." Josh fanned out the tickets and wiggled an eyebrow in Sailor's direction. "Doing anything tonight, Miss Kern?"

❧

Sailor made a quick trip home to change, and an hour later the Fannings picked her up for the drive to Branson. As she followed Josh and Deb down the aisle to their theater seats, she stifled a delighted shiver. She hadn't expected her secret gift would garner an invitation to attend with them. The Fannings had brought her to a Frankie Verona show for her eighteenth birthday, and she and her friend Kathy enjoyed the occasional weekend getaway to see other Branson performers. Andy Williams, the Lennon Sisters, Dolly Parton's Dixie Stampede—sometimes Sailor couldn't believe she lived only a few miles up the highway from so many classic entertainers.

Tonight, however, would be her first time to experience the up-close-and-personal thrill of a front-row seat. Faux starlight twinkled in the arched blue ceiling. A simulated harvest moon shimmered above the maroon velvet stage curtain. The hivelike hum of anticipation grew louder as the theater filled for the eight o'clock show.

A timpani fanfare silenced the auditorium, and an announcer's voice reverberated overhead: "Ladies and gentlemen, welcome to Frankie Verona's Moonlight over Missouri Theater!"

The lights went down, the curtain rose, and a live stage band picked up the strains of Frankie's theme song. Three ladies in sequined ankle-length gowns swayed in unison as they harmonized to the opening lines. Then Frankie Verona himself strode onstage in a gem-encrusted tux, his ink black hair slicked into a pompadour. The audience applauded and cheered, its enthusiasm sweeping Sailor along until she found herself clapping so hard her palms stung.

It didn't matter that sitting this close she could see every line and wrinkle in the aging entertainer's face. Frankie remained the consummate performer, his voice as strong and resonant as on Josh and Deb's CDs. The syncopated rhythm and reflected glow from the stage lights wrapped around Sailor, filling her, lifting her, making her feel as though Frankie sang only to her.

When the opening number came to an end, she finally found a full breath. She sank into her seat cushion and sighed.

"Isn't he incredible?" Deb squeezed her hand.

Sailor squeezed back. "Amazing! Thanks for bringing me."

"Good evening, Missouri lovers!" Frankie stepped to the front of the stage, so close that Sailor could almost look up his nostrils. His tux sparkled under red, blue, and amber spotlights. "So glad you could join me tonight. Let me introduce my wonderful singers and musicians. Singing lead soprano, the lovely Laura Travis."

A statuesque woman took one step forward and bowed slightly from the waist, the spotlight bringing out red highlights in her upswept hair. If not for the fancy dress and stage makeup. . .

Sailor grabbed Deb's arm. "Oh my goodness, that's my dental hygienist!"

"From Dr. Simpson's office—you're right." Deb elbowed Josh. "Did you know she sang?"

Sailor lost Josh's response to a surge of applause. She missed the names of the other two backup singers and strained to catch Frankie's introduction of the musicians, beginning with the drummer, bass guitarist, keyboard player, saxophonist, and finally—

Sailor's eyes popped open. She hardly recognized the man in black leather jeans and a silver satin shirt with softly billowing sleeves. Ash brown hair curled over his ears and shirt collar. A boyish grin lit his face when he stepped forward to take his bow.

The gray green gaze met Sailor's, and her stomach plummeted to her toes.

❧

"And last but not least, Parker Travis on flute. My special thanks to Parker for stepping in at the last minute after our regular flutist became ill. And did I mention the lovely Laura is his gorgeous and talented mom?"

Parker tore his gaze from the stunned face of the girl in the front row and hoped his own surprise didn't show. Sailor Kern, here tonight? *Look, Lord, I know I've been avoiding the whole boy-meets-girl thing. You trying to tell me something here?*

Gathering his wits, he acknowledged the applause with a nod and a quick kiss on his mother's cheek. Before returning to his position, he cast a nervous grin toward the wings, where Grams watched from a plush recliner. A flutist in a Branson show band herself before rheumatoid arthritis destroyed her fingers, she never missed her daughter's performances if she could help it.

Parker's gut clenched. If he ever found out Grams had anything to do with Sailor Kern showing up in the audience, they'd have to have a serious talk about boundaries.

Somehow he made it through the next couple of numbers but only with the firm resolve not to lower his glance to the first row, center section. Unfortunately his eyes wouldn't co-operate. Halfway through "Love Me Baby" he glimpsed the sharp-looking guy sitting next to Sailor, and the way they laughed and tilted their heads together gave every indication they were more than casual acquaintances.

Way more.

He had no right to be this bothered that his pretty little water aerobics instructor had a date. All he knew was that Sailor Kern evoked something inside him that he'd never allowed himself to feel before, and he had no clue what to do with it.

Two hours later, when the curtain closed after a couple of encores and their final bows, his breath whooshed out in relief. Playing for friends and family at church services was one thing. Performing onstage with a jazz legend while dealing with an unexpected attraction to a girl who clearly had eyes for someone else. . . *Lord, help!*

His mother grabbed his elbow as he ran the cleaning cloth through a section of his flute. "Do that later. Frankie's waiting for us."

"For what?"

Mom gave him one of her get-your-act-together looks. "You know—time to mingle with the audience and sign autographs."

"I'm only a sub. Nobody's here to see me." Anyway, if he stalled backstage long enough, maybe Sailor and her date would be long gone.

"Oh, just come on. Bask in the glory."

Following his mother out front, he spotted Sailor and her guy with an older couple, all surrounding Frankie while he chatted with them and signed their programs.

Frankie waved a hand, his gold rings flashing. "Laura, Parker, come say hello to these nice folks. They say they know you."

The tall woman with the carrottop extended her hand to Parker's mother. "Hi, Laura! Deb Fanning. You cleaned my teeth once when I couldn't get an appointment with my regular dentist. If I had any idea you sang with Frankie, I'd have been bugging you for tickets."

Parker's mother bumped shoulders with Mrs. Fanning and gave a meaningful smile. "Exactly why I don't make a big deal of it."

"Oops, good point." Mrs. Fanning cast a smile in Parker's direction. "So this handsome flute player is your son. Our friend Sailor tells me he's also in her water aerobics class."

"Sailor, how *wonderful* to see you here!" Parker's mom seized Sailor's hand as if greeting a long-lost relative. "My, my, it's one coincidence after another."

Parker hooked his thumbs in his back pockets. "No kidding."

"Just like old home week, eh?" Frankie Verona handed back their programs and excused himself to mingle with the other audience members.

The silver-haired Mr. Fanning took a half step back. "Well, we shouldn't keep you. . . ."

"Oh no, it's perfectly okay." Parker's mother linked her arm through Sailor's. "I'm dying to hear how Parker's doing in your class."

Sailor glanced at her date, who edged sideways as if to avoid the pushy woman in sequins. "He's, um—"

"Mom, we should go check on Grams, huh?" Parker aimed one foot toward the stage.

"She's fine, having her usual cup of chamomile with the makeup lady. Now, Sailor," she went on, drawing the wide-eyed girl to one side. "By the way, did I ever tell you what a beautiful name you have? I'm thrilled Parker's taking your class. He works way too hard, you know."

They moved out of earshot, leaving Parker shuffling his feet next to the Fanning couple and the wimp who wouldn't lift a hand to rescue his girl from the clutches of Parker's meddling mother. He searched for something to say. "So you're all friends of Sailor's?"

Mrs. Fanning nodded. "We've known her since she was a

teenager. She used to babysit for our rowdy bunch of sons. Right, Tom?" She elbowed Sailor's date.

"Mo–om." The red-faced guy grimaced and rolled his eyes.

Parker palmed a sudden pinch under his ribcage. "Sailor babysat *you*?"

"Guilty as charged." Tom—Tom Fanning, apparently—flashed a pearly grin, and for the first time Parker could tell he was much younger than he first thought, probably midtwenties at most. "But don't believe anything she says about me. And for heaven's sake don't repeat it to my wife. She still thinks I'm Mr. Totally Cool."

"You're married." Parker felt a silly smile creep across his face. "So you and Sailor aren't. . ."

"Are you kidding? No way!" Tom's eyes crinkled. "Sailor only came with us because some stranger gave my folks four tickets and my wife had to go to a baby shower."

"Some stranger?" Parker glanced toward the wings, imagining Grams smugly sipping her chamomile. No. Not possible. How could she possibly have known the Fannings would bring Sailor to the show?

Paranoia, thy name is Parker.

five

Sailor heaved a reluctant sigh and dropped *Love's Sweet Song* into the book return. "Alas, farewell, my love. 'Twas such sweet agony sharing these past few days with you."

"Spare me!" Kathy pressed the back of one hand to her forehead. She might be teasing, but her tone sounded noticeably edgier than normal.

Had she been listening to the rumors about Chandler's "bad boy" past?

Kathy retrieved the book and scanned it in. "Two weeks to the day. How many times did you read it?"

"Only three." Sailor lowered her eyes. "Four, if you count skimming for all the best romantic scenes."

"Wow, a new all-time low. Didn't you read his last one six times before returning it? And three days late, if memory serves."

"I've had a busy couple of weeks." Sailor propped an elbow on the counter. "See, this so-called *friend* coerced me into being on her committee."

"Hmm, would that be the same friend who made you Chandler Michaels's official Bards of Birkenstock social director?" Kathy set a stack of returned books on the counter and began scanning them. "And since we've only had two meetings since you joined the committee, you must have some other reason for staying so busy."

"My classes *have* been a little more draining than usual. And I spent Saturday with the Fannings. They took me to a Frankie Verona show."

"In Branson? Cool!"

A funny ripple rolled up her spine. "Guess who was in the band, subbing for the regular flute player."

Kathy shrugged and scanned in another book.

"My new student. Parker Travis."

"Seriously? How cool!" Kathy's eyes narrowed. "Why, Sailor Kern, what's that look I see on your face? Please tell me you're about to give up this Chandler Michaels infatuation and set your cap for Birkenstock's premier hairstylist instead."

"No!" Sailor hugged herself against a sudden shiver. No, she most definitely was *not* interested in Parker Travis. "I'm trying to get up the nerve to make an appointment. You know, so I look my best for the festival."

As Kathy's gaze drifted toward the entrance, her brows shot up. "Here's your chance."

"Huh?" Sailor swiveled to see the hairstylist in question ambling across the lobby. Her mouth dropped open. He hesitated long enough for her to clamp her teeth together and force a smile.

"Hi again." Parker edged toward the counter and stuffed his hands into his pockets. "Hope you enjoyed the show the other night. Sorry if my mom monopolized you."

Sailor recalled Mrs. Travis's probing questions and lifted one shoulder. "She was just being a mom." *As if I would know.* If not for Deb Fanning, she wouldn't have much of a clue about how real mothers acted.

But come to think of it, Deb had acted pretty motherly the other night, too. Like she and Mrs. Travis were trying to match up their "kids."

Her stomach lurched. She crossed her arms. "Anyway, you were great. I mean, Frankie was great. The *show* was great. It was all. . .great."

"I think he got the 'great' part." Kathy angled a smile toward Parker. "Hi, I'm Kathy, Sailor's very best friend."

Parker did a double take. "Kathy Richmond? Weren't we in band together? Flute, right?"

"I was a lowly freshman, and you were already first chair as a sophomore. I was so intimidated."

"Yeah, right," Parker smirked. "Didn't you drop out of band?"

"Halfway through the first semester. Passed out on the field during marching practice and never went back." Kathy straightened a stack of complimentary bookmarks. "I don't think I've seen you in the library before."

Parker's glance shifted between Kathy and Sailor. "It's my day off, and I just thought I'd. . .come in and look around. . . ."

Sailor's eyes narrowed to slits. People did not simply drop in at the library to "look around." Especially classy flute-playing hairstylists who most likely had a billion other, more interesting things to do. Like maybe style some famous person's hair or rehearse for another Branson show.

Sailor decided it was none of her business. Anyway, she didn't want to hang around and risk reinserting foot in mouth. More like foot, ankle, calf, and knee. "I should probably go. I need to find another book."

"But isn't there something you wanted to ask Parker?" Kathy wiggled her eyebrows meaningfully.

"Oh." Sailor gulped. She slid the toe of her sneaker across a beige floor tile, following the swirl in the design. "I. . .I was thinking about doing something different with my hair."

"Really?" Parker's voice softened in a way that sent tingles across Sailor's shoulders. "I'd be glad to help. Just call the salon and make an appointment."

Something lightened deep within her, like cola fizz finding its way to the surface of a shaken two-liter bottle. "Okay, I will."

❧

Parker became aware of one corner of his mouth curling upward as he watched Sailor scurry toward the shelves. She disappeared between A–F and G–M of the romance section at the same moment he heard the sound of a tornado blowing through—his own explosive sigh. He cringed.

"Packs quite a punch for as quiet as she is, huh?"

Parker jerked his head toward Kathy. "What?"

"Sailor. Most people never look beyond her shyness." She shot him a grin that punched a hole in his gut. "But I can tell you already have."

He stepped up to the counter. "Have you known Sailor long?"

"I was the resident assistant in our Missouri State dorm in Springfield when she was an incoming freshman." Kathy leaned forward, forearms resting on the counter. "So what are your intentions toward Sailor Kern?"

"Intentions?" Parker sucked in a quick breath then blew it out slowly. "All I know is, she throws me way off balance."

Kathy studied Parker as if she were sizing him up for a straitjacket. She slid a furtive glance toward the rows of bookshelves. "If you really are interested in Sailor, you should know something. She's got a megacrush on her favorite romance novelist, and she isn't going to get over him without a fight."

Kathy's concerned frown told him she was anything but happy about this so-called crush. "Who is this guy? Are they seeing each other?"

"They haven't met—yet." Another visual sweep of the bookshelves. "But he's coming to town for the Bards of Birkenstock Festival, and idiot that I am, I invited Sailor to be on the committee."

"Does this have anything to do with her sudden interest in getting a makeover?"

"You guessed it."

Parker scratched an imaginary itch along his jaw and stared off in the direction Sailor had disappeared to. "But she's gorgeous just the way she is." His mouth went dry. Did he *really* just say that out loud?

"I completely agree. I ask God every day to help her believe it for herself." Kathy paused to help another library patron check out a stack of books. Finishing, she returned her attention to Parker. "You never said. Is there a particular book you're looking for?"

Just what he needed—letting a casual acquaintance see how unnerved his growing attraction to Sailor had made him. He massaged the back of his neck. "The thing is, I'm a little out of practice in this whole. . .relationship thing."

Out of practice? How about completely out of touch? His last real date was probably the night he took second-chair flutist Marie Zipp to their high school band banquet. Just because most of his clients were female didn't give him any advantages in the romance department. And face it, no woman he'd met thus far had even come close to capturing his heart.

Until Sailor.

"So. . .you came to the library in search of a book on relationships." Kathy drummed her fingers on the counter. "May I assume you mean something a little deeper than friendship?"

Parker swallowed. "You may assume."

A grin spread across her wide mouth, a grin that looked more Machiavellian than friendly. "I have exactly the book you need."

Motioning for one of the other librarians to cover the front desk, Kathy reached for something on a lower shelf. She tucked a slim, shiny paperback under her arm, stepped through a swinging gate, and hurried Parker to one of the study carrels behind the reference section.

"Have a seat, Parker, and prepare to be enlightened." She took a chair across the narrow table from him and laid the book between them. "The library got in a shipment of advance review copies a few days ago, and when I came across this one, I squirreled it away before anyone else could grab it. I'm betting it'll give you exactly the ammunition you'll need to woo Sailor away from her fantasy man."

He studied the silhouetted couple on the cover, their lips meeting for a kiss in the center of a stylized red heart. "*Romance by the Book*, eh? So simple even a dork like me can learn?"

"Haven't you heard the rumors?" Kathy gave a low chuckle. "Word on the street is, you're the most eligible bachelor in

Birkenstock."

Parker flinched. "Guess I'm hanging out on the wrong street corners."

"Or maybe you haven't been paying attention." Kathy crossed her arms and waited while Parker paged through the book.

The first few chapter headings seemed straightforward enough. "What to Say after You Say Hello." "Make Your First Date First-Rate." "You Can't Go Wrong with Roses." "What to Do When 'Like' Turns to 'Love.'"

Okay, maybe he was still in the "like" phase with Sailor. But the incessant pounding behind his sternum every time he was around her—or even thought about her, truth be told—had him wondering if she was the girl he'd been holding out for his entire life.

He flipped the book over and scanned the back-cover blurb and author's photo. The guy in the white dinner jacket reminded him of an aging Daniel Craig straight from a James Bond movie. "Chandler Michaels. So he knows about this romance stuff, right?"

Kathy gave a doubtful huff. "That's what he claims."

"Wait. You recommended this book."

She did a slow eye roll. "What I said was, it'll give you the ammunition you'll need to beat the man at his own game."

Understanding dawned. Parker whistled through his teeth. "You mean this guy"—he knuckled the photo of Chandler Michaels—"is the author she has a crush on?"

"You got it." Kathy's jaw tensed. She gave her head an annoyed shake. "Ever hear of a BHS alum named Chuck Michalicek?"

The name settled like a block of ice in the center of Parker's chest. "Chuck Michalicek is Chandler Michaels?"

"One and the same." Kathy checked her watch and stood. "I have to get back to the desk. Just take the book and read it. You'll get the picture."

Alone in the carrel, Parker stared at the photo of Chandler

Michaels while the urge to hit something writhed beneath his rib cage. He'd been only eight or nine at the time, but he could still remember crouching on the stairs, listening to his mother trying to comfort her younger sister, his aunt Ruthy, after her fiancé ditched her two days before their wedding. They'd gotten engaged right out of high school, but the guy left soon afterward to attend an out-of-state college. Turned out he was cheating on Ruthy the entire time they were apart, and it was a blessing she didn't end up married to the creep.

A creep named Chuck Michalicek.

six

Sailor drew a chair up to the conference table and clicked the button on her ballpoint. She stared at the blank yellow legal pad before her. Guilt plagued her—not a single new idea of her own for Chandler's stay in Birkenstock. If she didn't prove she could make a valuable contribution to this committee, they might decide to vote her off.

Her practical side, the part intent on self-preservation at all costs, thought that might not be such a bad thing.

Her romantic side—sorely neglected except for a steady diet of romance novels—screamed ugly threats at her for even considering backing out of this once-in-a-lifetime opportunity.

The conference room door swung open, and Kathy breezed in. "Hey, Sailor, you're early. The meeting doesn't start for another twenty minutes—and that's only if Donna shows up on time."

She swiveled her chair around and pulled the legal pad into her lap, propping it on her knee so Kathy couldn't see the blank page. "Just doing a little brainstorming for Chandler's visit."

"Come up with anything interesting? Like maybe a necktie party?"

"Kathy!"

"Did I say necktie? I meant *black* tie." Kathy began aligning chairs and setting out extra notepads and pens.

Sailor rotated her chair to follow Kathy's movements. She jotted numbers one through ten in the left margin then tapped her pen on the first line. "At the last meeting you mentioned taking him to a Branson show. I bet I can get more tickets to see Frankie Verona."

"Good idea. They're from around the same era. Oldies but goodies and all." Kathy checked the thermostat and made a small adjustment.

Sailor smirked. Nothing subtle about Kathy Richmond. "I'm sure Frankie's got several years on Chandler. Remember, I had a front-row seat the other night. Stage makeup covers a multitude of. . .wrinkles."

Kathy plopped into the chair next to Sailor's, her dark hair puffing out around her shoulders. She sat forward and gripped Sailor's armrests. "What's it going to take for you to realize you deserve someone way better, not to mention *younger*, than Chuck Michalicek?"

Resentment pricked Sailor's spine. "Age is only a number. And what's it going to take for you to realize maybe a guy can change? Isn't it possible Chandler. . .Chuck—whatever you want to call him—has moved beyond the silly pranks he pulled as a teenager?"

Kathy straightened. "I gather I'm not the only one who's been talking to you about Chuck."

"I've heard a few rumors." Sailor hugged the legal pad against her chest. "But that's all they are—rumors. And anyway, doesn't it say in the Bible that we're all new creations in Christ? How do you know Chandler hasn't changed?"

"How do you know he has? Or that he's even a Christian?"

"I'm giving him the benefit of the doubt. Isn't that what good Christians are supposed to do?"

Kathy narrowed one eye. "I'm starting to really worry about you, Sailor. And I don't mean only where Chandler Michaels is concerned."

Sailor stiffened. "Why?"

"I've had this sense lately that you and God are. . .well, not as close as you ought to be."

Sailor sucked her lower lip between her teeth. The truth stung, and she couldn't stop her next words. "I don't think my relationship with the Lord is any of your business."

Kathy's chin lifted. Hurt shimmered in her deep brown eyes. "I'm your friend, Sailor. That should be plenty of reason—"

"Good evening, ladies." The white-haired Allan Biltmore

waltzed into the room and pulled out the chair on Sailor's other side. "You two have the privilege of being the first to hear my exciting news."

Sailor smiled a silent apology to Kathy—she knew her friend only spoke out of concern—and folded her hands atop the legal pad as she swiveled toward Allan.

Behind her she heard Kathy's sharp exhalation and the forced smile in her voice. "What's up, Allan?"

"Did I mention I was Chandler Michaels's high school English teacher?" He chuckled softly. "Of course I knew him as Charles back then, and indeed he was a live wire. How well I remember—"

"Your news, Allan?" Kathy scooted her chair closer and propped one elbow on the table.

"Ah yes, I digress. Since Charles—Chandler—will be staying with me, we've been in touch about his travel plans." Allan's grin broadened to reveal a set of pearly false teeth. "You, my dear Sailor, are going to be one busy young lady. It turns out Chandler is so thrilled about returning to Birkenstock for this momentous occasion that he has decided to move up his arrival. He'll be coming to town next week."

"N—next *week*?" Nausea seethed up Sailor's esophagus. Should she be thrilled? Terrified? Catch the next bus out of town?

"Wow, Allan, that's. . .amazing." Kathy's voice held an edge that only increased Sailor's panic. A hand reached over the back of Sailor's chair and squeezed her shoulder.

"Indeed. However, Chandler will have some special requirements that—" The arrival of three more committee members interrupted Allan's explanation, and he couldn't resist boasting to the others about this little coup.

Soon the entire committee had assembled, and the louder the conversational hum became, the deeper Sailor withdrew inside herself. Donna DuPont called the meeting to order, and though Sailor tried to look interested and take notes as the chairwoman worked through the agenda, her mind wouldn't cooperate. Soon she'd be asked to give a report on her ideas for keeping Chandler Michaels entertained, and Allan Biltmore's announcement had thrown a megasized monkey wrench into the mix. Nearly four extra weeks to fill? Not to mention Chandler's "special requirements"! Allan explained that Chandler had asked him to keep the details confidential for now, but that everything was under control. Still. . .what exactly would Chandler expect of her?

God, are You there?

No answer.

I know Kathy's right. You and I haven't really talked in ages. But I'm in trouble here. The chance to meet Chandler Michaels is the most wonderful, exciting thing that's ever happened to me. How will I ever be ready by next week?. . . God?

Still nothing.

And Donna DuPont was looking her way.

❧

"Thanks for working me in, Parker." Donna DuPont fluffed the black protective cape over her knees as Parker secured the Velcro closure around her neck. "Howard and I are hosting a dinner party tonight for the city council members, and I want to look my best."

"Have no fear, your favorite stylist is here." Parker cupped his hands around Donna's hair and pushed it one way and then another. "I'm thinking a little upsweep on the left side to play up those classy pearl earrings Howard bought you in Maui."

"You remembered." She winked at him through the mirror. "And I thought all my babbling went in one ear and out the other."

Sometimes he wished it did. There were days he'd like to remind his clients he was their hairstylist, not a gossip columnist. Or worse, their shrink. . .although he firmly believed what he did for his clients gave their self-esteem a bigger boost than any psychiatrist could ever hope for.

Could he do the same for Sailor Kern?

He wished she'd call. It was Thursday already, not that he was keeping track. Tuesday at the water aerobics class, things had seemed awkward between them, at least from his perspective. She remained all business, unflappable beneath her instructor persona, never even mentioning their encounter at the library.

And of course he wasn't about to mention his reason for being at the library in the first place. Or the fact that her interest in the infamous Chuck Michalicek aka Chandler Michaels had him spitting nails—and not the acrylic kind.

"Parker? Yoo-hoo, Parker Travis!" Donna's singsong voice interrupted his thoughts.

"Sorry, let's get you over to the shampoo bowl."

"What has you so preoccupied lately?"

Parker guided her head into the bowl and tested the water. "Just a little concerned about a friend." *Friend?* His stomach clenched at the realization of how badly he wanted it to be more. Somewhere along the way, he'd ceased resigning himself to bachelorhood and started tripping over his own feet in the presence of one excruciatingly naive and unbearably beautiful woman.

Donna wriggled her bottom deeper into the chair and closed her eyes. "As often as I've confided my secrets to you, you can certainly unburden yourself to me if you feel like it. I'm all ears, honey."

"Thanks, but this isn't something I can talk about." He squirted her favorite peach-scented shampoo into his palm and massaged it into mounds of foam.

He'd just rinsed out the shampoo and applied conditioner when Carla, the receptionist, pranced over, a loose-fitting leopard-print tunic swishing around her thighs. "Can you take a call, Parker? I've got a gal on the line who will only speak with you."

Great, probably another client who'd insist on being worked in before the weekend. His schedule was already jam-packed. At this rate, whatever pain relief the water aerobics class provided would soon be undone. Even with only sporadic attempts to practice on his own, neither his shoulders nor his knees had felt this good in a long time.

He chewed the inside of his cheek. "Let me get Donna to my station, and I'll pick up there."

Donna sat up and adjusted the towel he had wrapped around her head. "Don't take long, honey. I've got to get home to let the caterers in."

"This will only take a second." As Donna settled into the chair, he grabbed the cordless extension from the wall base. "Parker here. How can I help you?"

"Um, hi. I hope this isn't a bad time. . . ."

His heart did a crazy spin and thud. He'd know that quiet voice anywhere. "No, not at all." He eyed Donna through the mirror then stepped around the corner and lowered his voice. "I've got all the time in the world." *For you.*

Silence stretched between them, and he started to wonder if he'd lost the connection. When she finally spoke, frantic desperation filled her tone. "Parker, you've *got* to help me. Everyone says you're the best stylist in town, and Chandler Michaels is coming *next week*, and I haven't done anything with my hair in years, and I look like. . .like. . ." She made a gurgling sound, like a sob catching in her throat. Then a huge, ragged sigh rasped out.

He wanted to tell her she looked like an angel. He wanted to tell her to stay far, far, far away from Chuck Michalicek. He wanted to tell her she deserved somebody with a lot more class. Somebody who would cherish her and love her just the way she was.

Somebody like him.

Donna tapped him on the shoulder. "My hair's drying all funny. Hurry up!"

He pasted on an obliging smile and motioned her back to the chair. Speaking into the phone, he said, "Can you come in Saturday at four? My last appointment is at three thirty. After that we can spend all the time you need."

"I'll be there." Relief thick as honey poured through the phone line. "Thank you so much!"

"You're more than welcome. 'Bye, Sailor." He set the phone in its base and reached for a comb.

"Sailor?" Donna quirked an eyebrow. "Not Sailor Kern? She's on my Bards of Birkenstock committee. Sweet little thing." She gave a tiny gasp, her mouth forming an O. "She made an appointment with you? All I can say is, it's about time. The poor girl's as plain as a country mouse."

Parker felt a pinch in his gut. "I don't think—"

"It was all I could do to keep from saying anything when Kathy Richmond invited her to help with the arrangements for Chandler Michaels's visit. Why, for goodness' sake, she hardly says a word at our meetings. I can't imagine her holding her own in a social setting, least of all with a literary luminary like—"

Parker flicked the blow-dryer switch to its highest setting. "Sorry, Donna, can't hear you over this noise."

Chuck Michalicek, *literary*? A celebrity, maybe. A legend in his own mind, for sure. Parker had spent the last couple of evenings skimming the contents of *Romance by the Book* and wondering what kind of slimeball would come up with this stuff.

An egotistical, womanizing, male-chauvinist slimeball, obviously. Whether Sailor ever looked twice in Parker's direction or not, he'd keep her away from Chuck Michalicek if he had to kidnap her and tie her up in the salon storeroom until the book festival ended and "Chandler Michaels" had left Birkenstock in the dust.

seven

Sailor angled her aging green Honda Civic into the only vacant parking space she could find along Willow Avenue, two blocks south of Par Excellence Salon and Day Spa. She tipped her head to check her reflection in the rearview mirror. As usual, several escapees from her perennial ponytail now drooped across one eye. Parker Travis had his work cut out for him.

She only hoped he didn't charge by the hour.

Slinging her back-friendly—but not so fashionable, she suddenly realized—handbag over one shoulder, she locked her car, fed the meter, and headed up the street. Three shops down from the salon she slowed her pace then drew up short next to a big blue mailbox at the curb. She swallowed the butterflies swarming her throat, not that she felt any better having them flutter around inside her stomach.

You can do this, Sailor. Keep your objective firmly in mind.

Dodging a couple of kids on skateboards, she tramped the rest of the way to the salon. With a final steadying breath she pushed through the amber-tinted glass door.

"Hi, can I help you?" A perky receptionist with asymmetrically cut blue black hair looked up from filing her nails. The brass plaque at one end of the counter indicated her name was Carla.

"I made—" Sailor cleared the squeak from her voice. "I made an appointment with Parker Travis. My name is—"

"Sailor Kern. Four o'clock." Carla ran a finger down her computer screen. "Parker's finishing up a lowlight. Can I get you a soda or some coffee while you wait?"

"No thanks." She glanced around the seating area and spied

a basket of hairstyle magazines. She scooped up the top three. "I'll just look through these."

"That first one's my favorite. It's chock-full of trendy styles." Carla came around and plopped onto the plush black leather sofa next to Sailor. She snatched the magazine and riffled through the pages, then she flipped it open on Sailor's lap and pointed to a photo. "The minute you walked in the door, I could *see* you in this 'do. I have a knack for these things, you know. Just show it to Parker, and he'll—"

"Thanks, Carla, I'll take it from here."

The sound of Parker's voice, strong and sure, sent nervous prickles up Sailor's arms. She jerked her head up to see him escort a sixty-something woman into the reception area. A stunning mass of bronze and golden waves set off the woman's warm complexion.

"Have a wonderful time at the theater tonight, Mary." He gave the woman a chaste peck on the cheek then signaled Carla over to the counter. "Would you please set Mrs. Blodgett up for another appointment in four weeks?"

Sailor rose, the magazine clutched against her abdomen. Parker seemed so different here than at the water aerobics class, or even when she ran into him at the library the other day. A confident grace marked both his posture and his tone, the complete opposite of his self-conscious bumbling while trying to master the pool exercises.

He turned to her, and she glimpsed the tiniest flicker of uncertainty in his awkward smile. It quickly vanished when he extended his hand. "Hi, Sailor. Come on back."

She followed him through a maze of styling cubicles, past a bay of hood-type hair dryers, and around a center atrium where an out-of-control ficus plant stretched its shedding limbs toward a skylight. A hallway branched to their right, and Sailor glimpsed a series of door signs: MANICURE/PEDICURE. FACIALS AND DEPILATORY. BODY TREATMENTS. MASSAGE.

"Wow, you do everything here." An envious sigh whispered

between her lips. It would take all those salon procedures and more to transform this plain-Jane nobody into drop-dead gorgeous. No use drooling over the impossible though. She'd probably have to work overtime for the next century to afford what Parker would charge for a simple cut and style.

Oh well, if it made the impression on Chandler Michaels she was hoping for, it would be worth every penny.

They arrived at a brightly lit cubicle with a window over-looking the street. Vertical blinds admitted soft sunlight upon a black-lacquered shelf covered with ferns, begonias, and English ivy. Forest-print wallpaper echoed the greenery and lent an airy, outdoorsy feel.

Parker motioned her into the chair and angled it toward the mirror. With a gentle touch he tugged the coated elastic band from her ponytail and combed his fingers through the strands until her hair flowed around her shoulders like a silken cur-tain. The sensation gave her chills. She breathed slowly in and out, a tremor vibrating deep in her throat.

"You have beautiful hair." Parker's voice held a mellow tone that matched the look in his eyes. He smiled at her through the mirror. "When was the last time you did anything to it?"

She bit her lip. "Well, I washed it this afternoon after I finished my lap swim."

"Other than shampooing, I mean." Parker fingered a strand. "I see just the slightest damage from pool chlorine. You must use a good conditioner."

"It's specially made for swimmers." Sailor smirked. "I may not know much about styling, but I do know I don't look good in green hair."

Parker shot her a knowing grin. "Do you trim it regularly? Have you ever used a coloring product? Had a perm?"

"My aunt Trina tried to give me a home perm for Easter Sunday one year, but it didn't take very well. Not to mention the smell."

"Ah yes, the ammonia. Perms have come a long way since

those days—not nearly so smelly and much kinder to the hair. Have you always worn your hair long?"

"Mostly. I like being able to pull it into a ponytail and not fuss with it." She grimaced. Nothing like admitting to a beauty professional that she avoided spending time on her appearance.

"Actually, an updo enhances your classic oval face." Parker smoothed her hair away from her temples and swept it up into a pile on the back of her head.

This time she couldn't suppress a visible shiver. The thought occurred to her that she could sit in this chair with Parker running his hands through her hair for the rest of their lives.

❧

Parker wasn't sure whether the sudden quiver up his arms originated in Sailor or himself. He only knew he'd like to spend the rest of his life running his fingers through her soft, silky tresses. He hadn't even needed to ask whether she'd used any kind of chemical process recently. Except for minor pool-related dryness at the ends, this was the cleanest, healthiest, most *un*processed hair he'd handled in a long, long time.

He pulled himself out of his self-indulgent reverie and recalled her real reason for being here: to make herself attractive for Chandler Michaels. His shoulders tightened. He squeezed out a sharp breath. "Okay, let's get started. Did you find a style you like in one of the magazines?"

"The receptionist was just showing me this one." The magazine fell open in Sailor's lap, revealing a photo of a model with purplish red hair cut long at the sides and tapering to a high V in back. Spiky bangs fringed her heavily made-up eyes. Judging from Sailor's sudden flinch as she glanced down, Parker guessed she hadn't looked closely at the photo until now.

He swept the magazine from her hands and tossed it onto the work space behind him. "Carla's taste leans toward the avant-garde. I had something more natural in mind for you."

Sailor released a thankful-sounding chuckle. "Just so it's

something I can manage on my own, especially with being in the water every day. I'm not real handy with a blow-dryer, and I wouldn't know what to do with gel or mousse or even a curling iron."

"I'll keep all that in mind." Parker ran a comb through her hair and pondered various styles, his sense of calling more powerful than ever. He'd felt the first inklings years ago, helping Grams brush out her tangles as rheumatoid arthritis slowly stole away her grip. "Thank you, Parker. You make me feel so pretty," she would say.

Now he had the chance to share this gift with the one person who most needed it, a woman who had not the slightest concept of how beautiful she really was. Yet if he helped her, he might send her straight into the arms of the one man who least deserved her affection.

His gut cramped. What choice did he have? She'd come to him expecting a makeover miracle, and he had the skill to give it to her.

He also had Chandler Michaels's treatise on romance tucked away in the bottom drawer. Obviously Kathy Richmond hadn't read it all the way through. If Sailor could be swayed by such corny macho tactics, maybe she was already too far gone.

"Think outside the box, Parker."

He tensed. Where had that thought come from?

"Think outside the book. *Trust Me."*

Sailor caught his eye in the mirror. "So do you have any ideas, or am I totally hopeless?"

"Hopeless? Not a chance." He laid the comb aside and rested his hands on her shoulders. "Do you trust me?"

She gulped. "I. . .I think so."

He gripped the sides of the chair and spun Sailor 180 degrees. Gasping, she clutched the chair arms and shot him a terrified look.

He grinned. "You said you trusted me, right?" At her wide-eyed nod, he continued. "Hold on to that thought then, because when you look in that mirror after we're finished today, you'll see Sailor Kern the way I see her. . . ."

He clamped his teeth together before he could add, *Beautiful beyond imagining.*

⌖

Sailor sucked in her breath as Parker swept around her, swirling a shimmery black cape like a matador. Beneath the slick fabric her fingers clawed the armrests. A thousand fire ants nibbled at her nerves. What was she thinking, putting herself at the mercy of a mad hairstylist? He must be mad if he thought he could change Sailor from an ugly duckling into Cinderella.

Or was she mixing up her fairy tales?

No matter. Nothing short of a fairy godmother could make her glamorous enough to attract the likes of Chandler Michaels. Besides, even if Parker succeeded in improving her outward appearance, sooner or later she would have to actually *talk* to Chandler. And when she opened her mouth and nothing came out but her typical shy little squeaks, her dream come true would turn into her worst nightmare.

Parker stood to one side, mixing something white and frothy in a square plastic container. The sharp smell bit at her sinuses. She put a finger beneath her nose. "Wh–what's that for?"

He laughed, a throaty, reassuring laugh—or at least she hoped he meant to be reassuring. "Don't panic. You promised you'd trust me."

Trust him? Oh man, that's what got her into this mess in the first place. When he pulled a stack of foil squares out of a drawer and moved toward her with something resembling a rattail paintbrush, she decided the wisest course of action would be to close her eyes and hope for the best.

She felt each stroke as he sectioned off her hair then tucked the foil close to her scalp. The scratchy brushing and crinkling sounds suggested he was painting on the white stuff then wrapping each strand in a neat little foil package. Part, tuck, brush, wrap. . .part, tuck, brush, wrap. . . . The rhythm lulled her into a languid calm.

"Sailor? You awake?" Parker jiggled her arm.

She popped her eyes open. "Sorry, I think I dozed off."

"Time for the next step. Come with me." With one hand on her shoulder, Parker guided her around the shedding ficus plant and down the hallway they'd passed earlier. The door to the manicure/pedicure room stood open, and Parker showed Sailor inside. He introduced her to a regal-looking woman seated behind a table.

"Nice to meet you, Sailor. I'm Pamela. Have a seat." A cap of reddish brown curls framed the woman's wide, exotic-looking eyes. She reached for Sailor's hand and studied the short nails.

Sailor's gaze skimmed the array of manicurist paraphernalia and bottles of polish in every shade imaginable. Painfully aware of her ragged cuticles and too-short nails, she wanted to jerk her hand back. "I've never had a professional manicure. But I guess that's pretty obvious." Not to mention she must look like a space alien or possibly a human TV antenna, with all that foil poking out around her head.

"First time for everything." The warmth in Pamela's coffee-brown gaze matched her tone. She slanted a grin in Parker's direction. "Go put your feet up for a while. I'll take good care of her."

The door clicked shut, and Sailor released a nervous chuckle. "I thought I was just here for a haircut. I hope the salon takes credit cards."

"Don't even think about money. This is your time to relax and enjoy." Pamela eased Sailor's fingers into a bowl of warm water. "Parker's been planning your appointment ever since you called. He's got all kinds of fun stuff lined up for you."

She gulped, a crazy mix of elation, anticipation, and stark terror rippling through her. Would she even recognize herself when Parker completed his work?

She couldn't wait to find out.

eight

Parker stretched one leg along the reception-area sofa and checked his watch—almost six. Sailor should be close to finishing her session with the makeup artist. He hoped Sandra followed his instructions to keep Sailor's look understated and natural.

He couldn't suppress a chuckle as he wondered how Sailor was handling all this special attention. She'd seemed more than slightly dumbstruck when he dropped her off for her mani/pedi. After she finished there, he brought her to the shampoo station to rinse out the highlighting solution and apply a deep conditioner. Then he'd sent her for a facial and eyebrow shaping. He'd debated scheduling a brown sugar scrub, full-body massage, and wardrobe consultation, but on such short notice and so late in the day, there wouldn't be time. Besides, he didn't want to completely overwhelm her. Maybe his selective introduction to pampering would encourage her to come back for more.

All that remained today was Parker's signature cut and style, and he knew exactly what he wanted to do. Subtle layering, a wisp of bangs, and the strategically placed highlights he'd applied earlier would set off Sailor's features beautifully.

He'd been trying all afternoon not to think about why he was doing this—or rather, for whom—but the image of Chandler Michaels gazing seductively from the back cover of his book wouldn't leave Parker alone. After the salon emptied out, and with Sailor ensconced with his skilled associates down the hall, he'd fished out the dreaded *Romance by the Book*. Might as well brush up on the competition.

The chapter that lay open before him made him want to gag: "Dressing Her for Success." Though the author cloaked his meaning in high-sounding prose and euphemisms, after two paragraphs Chandler Michaels's definition of *success* became crystal clear. The intervening years hadn't changed bad-boy Chuck in the slightest. Parker had the sick feeling that giving Sailor a makeover might only be playing into Chuck's hands—although he doubted a guy like Chuck could ever truly appreciate the unadorned beauty and artless charm of a woman like Sailor.

He closed his eyes and gave his head a helpless shake. *Lord, protect her.*

Footsteps clicking on the marble floor drew his attention. He slammed the book closed and tucked it beneath a sofa cushion as Sandra entered the reception area. She swept long blond waves off one shoulder. "All done. I sent her back to your station."

Parker stood. "How'd it go?"

"I did exactly what you asked. Mineral makeup in natural shades, and the lightest touch possible. I think you'll be suitably impressed." Sandra offered a sly smile. "She sure seemed to be."

Sandra's words buoyed Parker's steps as he headed through the salon. He found Sailor admiring her own reflection. Seeing him in the mirror, she brightened.

He grinned. As usual, Sandra's expertise proved flawless. "So far, so good?"

"I never realized what a difference a little makeup could make. And Sandra made it easy enough that I think I can actually learn to do it myself. She even gave me a product list and some samples."

Was she sitting a little straighter, her smile a tad more self-assured? He tugged the towel loose from around her hair and swiveled her away from the mirror once more.

She grabbed his wrist. "Hey, I trusted you through all this other stuff. Can't I watch while you do my hair?"

He shook off her hand and reached for a spray bottle to

dampen her towel-blotted tresses. "Nope. I want you to be surprised."

"Today has already been full of surprises." Her tone became pleading. "Come on, Parker, let me watch."

He couldn't help but laugh. "When did my Simon Legree water aerobics instructor become such a whiner?"

If a little makeup and nail polish could produce this much spunk, he couldn't wait to see how she'd react when she saw the finished product.

❧

When Parker laid the dryer and brush aside and reached for a can of hair spray, Sailor clamped her eyes shut. A fruity scent lingered in the air as the light mist tickled her nose. When Parker whisked away the protective cape and rotated the chair toward the mirror, she shivered, afraid to open her eyes.

"You might as well look and get it over with." His voice rang with self-satisfaction. The guy was good, and he obviously knew it.

So why was she so afraid? It had nothing to do with Parker Travis's hairstyling skills.

It had everything to do with her doubts that she could live up to a new-and-improved version of herself. Who would she be when she walked out the front door? Who did she *want* to be?

She drew in a deep breath, exhaled slowly, and willed her eyes to open. "Oh. My. Goodness."

Parker gave her a hand mirror and turned the chair so she could see the style from all angles. "Just enough layering to give some lift but still long enough for your ponytail. I added the highlights to enhance the golden undertones and brighten your face."

"Everything looks so. . .natural. Totally me, only better." Using her toe, she turned the chair toward the mirror again. She wanted to drink up the image before her.

Then reality hit. Her shoulders caved, and she groped for

her purse. "I should have asked sooner. How much is all this going to cost?"

Parker stepped between her and the hook where her purse hung. "This was entirely my pleasure. Everything's on the house."

"I can't let you do that." She dodged around him and swept her purse into her lap. "Seriously. How much do I owe you?"

"Don't argue, Sailor. I guarantee I'll win." He plopped into a forest green leather side chair, a smug smile twisting his lips. "The look on your face when you saw yourself just now is all the payment I need."

Her heart lifted in a series of staccato beats. Something in the way Parker was staring at her made her insides go all fizzy. She'd caught a similar look in his eyes during their last water aerobics class. Today, though, the intensity rocked her.

She gave herself a mental shake. Probably nothing but an overreaction to her very first spa day and the fact that for the first time in her life, a man was actually paying attention to her. A heady sensation, to be sure. But she'd better keep her eye on the real prize and hope the new Sailor Kern would attract equal attention from Chandler Michaels.

Giving an exaggerated eye roll, she unzipped her purse and retrieved her wallet. "Please let me pay you something, Parker. Otherwise I'll feel indebted to you for the rest of my life."

He chuckled and raised his hands in surrender. "Okay, okay. Here's my final offer. Since you only asked for a cut and style, that's all I'll charge you for—but of course you get my special discount for friends." He quoted an amount that still seemed on the high side.

She reminded herself he was the best, after all. "But what about Pamela and Sandra? Not to mention the products they used."

Parker rubbed his jaw and studied the ceiling. "You into bartering?"

"What exactly did you have in mind?"

"A few private water aerobics sessions ought to cover your spa services." His eyebrows drew up in the center, giving him a hopeful, little-boy look. "I mean it, there's a lot more to the workouts than I expected. I could really use some one-on-one coaching."

There went her heart again. What was wrong with her? She tapped her charge card against her chin. Her gaze slid to the mirror, and a fresh wave of confidence swept through her. "It would have to be in the evenings. Daytime hours are pretty much taken up with my classes and office work."

"Suits me. When shall we start?"

※

Who'd have thought finagling more face time with Sailor could be so easy? Parker mentally patted himself on the back as he shut off the salon lights and locked the front door behind him. It was after eight, the sidewalks of Birkenstock bathed in the pink gold glow of sunset. He found himself whistling on his way across the street to the public lot where he parked his Camry.

Halfway to the car he felt his cell phone vibrate and retrieved it from his pants pocket. The screen displayed the name Katherine Richmond. Oh yeah, Kathy the librarian. "Hi, Kathy. What's up?"

"Sailor just left my house. She couldn't wait to show me her new look. I had to call and tell you how. . .how. . ." Something between a groan and a squeal sliced through his eardrum. "Wow!"

He grinned and pumped one fist, unable to resist a moment of prideful gloating. "I take it you approve?"

"More than approve. I am totally amazed, astonished, and astounded. What you've done for that girl's self-esteem today is immeasurable."

"Then I've done my job. Except. . ." His stomach twisted. "The thought of her with Chuck Michalicek—"

"I know. Have you read the book?"

"Some." Parker tugged the small paperback from the pocket

of his Windbreaker and held it to the light. "He is one ego-maniacal skunk. And this stuff is supposed to *help* me keep Sailor away from him?"

Kathy was silent for a moment, a thoughtful sigh hissing through the phone. "I didn't have time to explain very well the other day. Could you meet me for coffee in twenty minutes?"

2&

Sailor breezed through the front door. "Hi, Uncle Ed. Sorry I'm so late. Did you find the dinner plate I left for you in the fridge?"

"You take real good care of me, sweetie." With a contented smile, her uncle glanced up from his book. "Did you get some supper?"

Reveling in her new look, she'd hardly even thought about being hungry, until her stomach chose that moment to utter a rolling growl. "Maybe I'll open a can of tuna and make myself a salad."

"Hold on, young lady." Uncle Ed reached for her hand and guided her around to the front of his chair. Removing his glasses, he scanned her up and down. "Something's different about you."

She shrugged and forced a smile. On her way home from Kathy's she'd started worrying about her uncle's reaction. Since she came to live with Uncle Ed and Aunt Trina, they'd tried to raise her as her ultraconservative parents expected. The Ogden and Hazel Kern Child-Rearing Manifesto consisted of six cardinal rules: church every Sunday, no rock music, only squeaky-clean TV programs, no makeup, no mini-skirts, and no dating until age eighteen.

Rock music had never appealed to her, and she'd always found books much more entertaining than TV (although she doubted her parents would be happy to know her reading tastes now centered on schmaltzy romances). Church every Sunday? Old habits were hard to break, even if God seemed distant these days. And with her tipping the scales at nearly

170 pounds by her eighteenth birthday, miniskirts were out of the question and dating was a nonissue. Makeup? Wouldn't have mattered anyway.

She flinched beneath her uncle's probing gaze. "Please, Uncle Ed, you're staring."

"Just trying to figure out what's changed." Finally one corner of his mouth curled upward. "You're wearing your hair down. Looks nice, real nice." He sat back with a satisfied sigh and returned his attention to his book.

The tension drained from Sailor's shoulders, replaced by a sense of elation. She recalled the approving look in Parker's eyes earlier. Now a similar reaction from her typically unobservant uncle? Never in her adult life had she felt so acutely aware of her womanhood.

Now the six-million-dollar question: Would Chandler Michaels notice?

nine

Parker arrived at Logan's Bistro a few minutes before Kathy. He claimed a table beneath a beaded lampshade that cast rippled blue shadows across the floor. When Kathy arrived, he waved her over and then placed their coffee orders with the barista. Returning to his chair, he slapped *Romance by the Book* on the table between them and snorted in disgust.

Kathy rolled her eyes. "My sentiments exactly."

"Has Sailor seen this book?"

"I told you, it's a review copy. Not in the bookstores yet, and Chandler hasn't even announced it on his Web site. Which is weird, if you ask me." She paused while the barista set their coffees on the table, then she took a cautious sip of her mocha latte. "Frankly, I hope Sailor *never* finds out about this book. It would break her heart."

Parker shot her a puzzled frown. "Wouldn't you want her to know the kind of guy she's harboring this misguided crush on?"

A sad sigh escaped Kathy's lips. "If you knew Sailor like I do, you'd understand. She's led an extremely sheltered life." Briefly she told him about Sailor's missionary parents and how for most of her childhood they had left her in the care of relatives. "After her aunt died, her world revolved around school and taking care of her uncle. Even at college I could hardly drag her away from the books. Social life? Forget it! She went home every weekend to check on her uncle. If not for the Fannings, she'd hardly know what having a real family is like."

Parker popped the spill-proof lid off his decaf cappuccino and swirled a wooden stir stick through the froth, releasing the brisk coffee aroma. "The Fannings. They brought her to the Branson show last weekend. Nice people."

"Very. But enough about Sailor's past. You and I need to concentrate on her future, and Chandler Michaels will be here next week."

"Yeah, Sailor said something about that when she made her appointment."

"It came as a surprise to everyone." Kathy leaned closer. "Remember Mr. Biltmore?"

"Senior English, third period. Hard to forget the teacher who gave me the one and only D of my high school career."

"You got a D in English? Really?"

"Let's keep this about Sailor, okay?" Parker crumpled his napkin. "What's Mr. Biltmore got to do with any of this?"

Kathy described Allan Biltmore's boastful announcement at the last committee meeting. "I guess ol' Chuck couldn't pass up the chance to extend his stay and bask in the glory—although what his 'special requirements' are is anybody's guess."

Parker grimaced. "After seeing this book, I don't even want to imagine."

"Why do I get the feeling your animosity stems from a lot more than reading a few chapters in his tacky how-to romance book?"

"Chuck and my family go way back. Let's leave it at that."

Kathy used the tip of one finger to push the book in a slow half circle. She stared at the cover and massaged her temples. "I don't get it. I've read several of Chandler Michaels's romance novels. They're all about virtuous heroines and gallant heroes finding true love. That he'd even write garbage like this just blows my mind."

Parker couldn't get the image of his brokenhearted aunt Ruthy out of his thoughts. "People will do all kinds of things for money."

"But his books top the bestseller lists regularly. He can't be that hard up for cash."

Frustration simmered in Parker's belly. He pushed his half-empty cup to one side and folded his hands on the table. "We can sit here and ruminate over Chuck's finances, or we can figure out how to keep Sailor from falling for his fake charm. When you suggested this meeting, I thought you were going to explain exactly how this book is supposed to help. Short of showing it to her so she can see Chuck Michalicek for the dog he is, I don't see any value in it whatsoever."

"Don't you understand? Sailor idolizes Chandler Michaels— or rather the romantic heartthrob she imagines him to be. I won't be the one to crush her dreams. I don't think you want that either." Kathy fisted one hand atop the book. "So use your head, Parker. Think outside the box."

The words knocked him backward like a punch to the sternum. *All right, Lord, You've got my attention.* He heaved a weary breath. "So what am I missing here? Obviously you have a plan in mind."

"Oh, you are dense, aren't you?" Kathy groaned. "No wonder you're pushing forty and still available."

"Hey, forty's a few years off yet. Get to the point, will you?"

"My point," Kathy said with a smirk, "is that if Chandler Michaels tries these tactics on Sailor, she'll see for herself what kind of guy he is."

"But won't that be even more devastating than just handing her the book?" Parker's gut clenched. "Not to mention more dangerous. Letting her actually spend time with him would be like sending her to the wolves—make that *wolf*."

"That's where you come in. While she's mooning over Chandler and escorting him to various writerly functions, you will be romancing her in true heroic fashion—doing the exact *opposite* of everything he describes in this book."

Parker couldn't stifle a pained laugh. "Now you're the one who's acting dense. In case you haven't figured it out, I don't have a romantic bone in my body."

Kathy drained the last of her latte and stood, hands braced on the table and her nose in Parker's face. "Then I suggest you go dig one up somewhere before Sailor rides off into the sunset on Chandler's not-so-lily-white steed."

❧

As the first glimmer of morning light filtered through her mini-blinds, Sailor's eyes popped open. Had she only dreamed the whole salon and spa experience? Hesitantly she touched her hair. Wispy bangs tickled her forehead. Soft layers brushed her cheeks. She sat up with a start and found her reflection in the dresser mirror. Even mussed from sleep, her hair fell across her shoulders in flattering lines.

"Wow," she told the image in the mirror, "you're looking pretty good there, girlfriend." She tilted her fingertips toward a sunbeam and admired the shiny, perfectly shaped nails.

Afraid she'd never be able to reproduce Parker's styling results without several practice sessions, she clipped her hair atop her head and tried not to get it damp during her morning shower. Afterward she made several attempts to match Sandra's light touch with the makeup brushes. Finally satisfied, she stood in front of her closet, pondering what to wear to church.

Her shoulders drooped at the meager choices. She'd definitely need a wardrobe update before she spent much time in Chandler's company. Opting for a khaki skirt and navy twinset, she finished dressing and hurried to the kitchen for a quick breakfast.

Uncle Ed turned toward her with the oversize brown coffee mug he'd just filled. Again he cocked his head as if trying to figure out what was different about her. She hoped she'd kept the makeup subtle enough that he wouldn't come unglued and report to her parents that their daughter was turning into a shameless hussy.

" 'Morning, Uncle Ed. Sleep well?" She busied herself preparing a bowl of organic wheat flakes.

"Fair to middlin'." He harrumphed. "How you can pour watery blue milk on that cardboard and call it breakfast is beyond me."

"I like skim milk." She carried the bowl to the table. "And the cereal is full of bran and nuts and flaxseed. It's good, really."

"And good *for* you, too," he mimicked. "You're mighty dressed up for work today."

His occasional mental lapses stabbed her heart. "It's Sunday, Uncle Ed. I'm dressed for church. You're always welcome to come along."

He muttered something unintelligible and carried his coffee to the living room.

Alone in the kitchen Sailor paused between bites and asked herself why she continued church attendance when her spiritual life seemed almost as dry as Uncle Ed's. Part of it was habit, of course. Part of it was obligation. How could she explain to Josh and Deb Fanning and her other friends at Mission Hills Bible Church that her relationship with God had been faltering for years?

If only she could understand why. Unlike Uncle Ed, she couldn't blame it on Aunt Trina's untimely death, and there'd been no other tragedies or upheavals to cause her to doubt God's love. No, hers had been a gradual drift, a cooling of the spiritual flame, a sense that though God was indeed out there somewhere He couldn't be bothered with a meek little mouse of a girl like Sailor.

The monstrous old black telephone jangled in the hallway. Startled, she dropped her spoon. On her way to the phone, she wished for the millionth time that her uncle wasn't so old-fashioned and antitechnology. Could it really hurt to subscribe to the caller ID service so she could at least prepare herself before picking up the receiver?

"Hi, Sailor. Didn't wake you, did I?" Deb Fanning sounded her usual cheery self.

Sailor smiled into the phone. "Are you kidding? I've been up since the crack of dawn."

"Should have known. Josh and I have to swing by the bakery to pick up doughnuts for our Sunday school class. We could pick you up on the way."

"Thanks, that's—" Sailor bit her lip. "Um, Deb, I just had this crazy idea." Crazy—and completely out of the blue. "I've been feeling a little. . .stale. . .in my attitude toward worship lately, and I was thinking it might help to visit some different churches, maybe get a fresh perspective."

Deb's soft breath whispered through the phone. "I've sensed for a while that you were struggling. I don't blame you a bit. Do you have someplace in mind?"

"Kathy's always told me I'd be welcome to attend with her." Then she remembered Kathy saying Lucille and Lorraine Douglas sang in the choir there. Nope, once a week with the Doublemint Twins was all Sailor could handle. "But I'm open to suggestions if you have any."

Deb remained quiet for a moment. "I've seen ads for a big church across town that looks interesting. Rejoice Fellowship, I think it's called. Josh told me the pastor is on the YMCA board of directors, and he likes him a lot."

The Fannings' recommendation was enough for Sailor. After saying good-bye to Deb, she looked up Rejoice Fellowship in the phone directory and called to ask the service times. Checking her watch, she found she could just make it for the ten-thirty worship.

The massive stucco sanctuary looked new. Narrow, beveled-glass windows framed the entrance and paraded around the hexagonal-shaped exterior. Sailor parked in a spot reserved for visitors, checked her reflection in the rearview mirror, and did a double take. Would she ever get used to seeing the new and improved version of herself?

As she exited the car, a young couple passed her on their way to the sanctuary. The woman, several months pregnant, paused and smiled over her shoulder. "Visiting? Glad to have you."

"Thanks." Sailor returned a quivery smile and fell in step with them on their way up the sidewalk.

"My name's Missy Underwood, and this is my husband,

Zach. Are you new to Birkenstock?"

"Um, no." It occurred to Sailor that she actually enjoyed being noticed. Feeling braver she introduced herself and confessed her need for a fresh perspective on worship.

"You'll definitely find that here," Zach said. "Rejoice Fellowship is a real Spirit-filled congregation."

Sailor's steps faltered briefly. Did she even know what it meant to be Spirit filled? An image of her parents slaving away on a new Bible translation flitted through her thoughts. Yes, they were dedicated workers for the Gospel. Yes, they always prayed openly and studied the scriptures. But Sailor wasn't sure even her very pious parents could be described as Spirit filled.

She was missing something—something vital. If what Zach said was true, maybe she would find it here.

She glanced up to see Zach holding open one of the broad double doors. As she and Missy stepped through to the marble and glass foyer, Missy cocked her head and gave Sailor a hard stare. "Wait a minute. I know you. Aren't you a patient of Dr. Ivan Simpson's?"

Sailor drew in her chin. "Dr. Simpson is my dentist."

"I'm a part-time hygienist there, but I just started my maternity leave." Missy's crystal laugh echoed in the cavernous foyer. "I'm not so good with names, but I'm usually better with faces. You look different with your hair down. I love it, by the way."

"Th–thank you." Sailor smoothed a flyaway strand and stood a little straighter.

"So you probably know Laura Travis, the other hygienist. She attends here, too." Missy started toward the sanctuary doors, where sounds from a praise band grew louder. "You'll sit with us, won't you?"

Sailor's feet felt superglued to the marble tile. If Laura Travis worshipped here, in all likelihood so did her son. The possibility of running into Parker sent Sailor's heart plunging to her toes.

Get over it, Sailor. She gave herself a mental shake and forced her legs into motion. Parker was her water aerobics student and now her hairstylist, nothing more. In only a few days she'd be face-to-face with Chandler Michaels, the man she'd been dreaming about since high school—ever since she fell in love with his book jacket photo on the back cover of *Love's Eternal Melody.*

ten

Parker gave his grandmother a kiss on her crinkly cheek, waved good-bye to the other sweet old gals at Willow Tree, and jogged out to the parking lot. With a grateful lift of his brow, he realized his knees hadn't felt this good in years—or his shoulders either. He checked his watch—just time to grab a root beer and burger at the Sonic drive-through, and then run home to scarf it down and change into his swim trunks before heading to the Y. Probably not the best idea to work out on a full stomach, but the hour between six and seven was all Sailor had available tonight for the extra coaching she'd promised him.

He still couldn't get over her showing up at church yesterday. Was the Lord intentionally bringing them together? *If that's true, Father, then You'll have to keep working on me.* Could he really hope to have it all—a successful business, his volunteer service at church and Willow Tree, looking after Mom and Grams, *and* true love?

Could he live with himself if he passed up the chance to find out?

He gulped down the rest of his burger, gave his teeth a thorough brushing, and swished with mouthwash. If he'd had his head on straight, he'd have asked the Sonic folks to hold the onions. Choosing not to chance Sailor's disapproval by showing up in cutoffs again, he tightened the string at the waist of those hideous orange swim trunks. He pulled an oversize gray T-shirt over his head, slid his feet into flip-flops, grabbed a towel, and headed out the door.

On the way to the Y, he mentally recapped the chapters he'd read last night in *Romance by the Book*. Clearly ol' Chuck was all about flash and dash. He'd devoted whole sections to choosing the perfect babe-magnet car, decorating the ideal bachelor pad, practicing tried-and-true come-on lines, setting the mood for the first kiss.

Parker grimaced. All the other stuff aside, he doubted he'd have to worry about a first kiss anytime soon. . .if ever.

Entering the pool area, he spotted Sailor finishing a mom-and-tot swim class. She climbed the steps behind a toddler in a flowery pink tank suit and bent to share a drippy hug. The sight made Parker's stomach clench. He clamped his lips together, marched across the deck, and wondered why his mouth had gone suddenly dry.

"Hi," he said hoarsely. One of Chandler Michaels's cheesier pickup lines came to mind, something about asking if she knew CPR because she took his breath away. He was almost tempted to use it.

"Perfect timing. Just let me get my gear." Sailor fastened a towel around her waist and started for the storage cabinet. Before she'd taken two steps toward him, she drew to a halt, her eyes the size of volleyballs. "Oh, my. No wonder you'd rather wear your cutoffs."

Heat shot up Parker's neck. He dropped his towel open and held it in front of him like a curtain. "I told you, Mabry's was a little low on choices. Believe me, I'll be shopping for another suit first chance I get."

Sailor's suppressed chuckle came out as a grunt. "Excuse me while I go get my sunglasses."

Since when did giving a girl a classy haircut turn her into Miss Snark? Had he created a monster? He tossed his towel, T-shirt, and flip-flops onto the bleachers, collected a set of workout gear from the cabinet, and slid into the water before he blinded too many innocent bystanders.

Dropping into the pool with barely a splash, Sailor offered a repentant grin. "Sorry for teasing you. Ready to get to work?"

The next hour was all business, Sailor's natural confidence in her teaching skills hiding every trace of insecurity. They finished the intense workout with a series of stretches. Parker heaved himself onto the deck and shook out arms that felt like rubber. "I apologize for ever thinking water aerobics was for wimps."

Sailor sat next to him on the edge of the pool. "I did work you a lot harder than I would most of my students." She grinned and aimed a splash at his midsection. "But I knew you could take it."

He splashed her back. "Thanks. I *think*."

She flicked water droplets off her cheek. "I was wondering. . ."

"Yeah?"

"Allan Biltmore is hosting a welcome dinner for Chandler Michaels this Friday, and I—"

Parker didn't realize his snort of disgust was audible until he caught Sailor's surprised glance. He scraped the back of his hand across his face. "Water in the nose. You were saying?"

"I'm worried about being able to get my hair to look as good as you did. I was hoping maybe you could. . .help."

"Do your hair for you? Sure, come by the shop Friday afternoon and I'll work you in. On the house, of course." He cast her a cockeyed grin and rubbed a tender calf muscle. "Consider it part of our trade agreement."

"That's really nice of you." Her shy vulnerability had crept back in, and it tugged at Parker's heart. He found himself staring at the curve of her lips and imagining what that first kiss would be like.

He cleared his throat and tore his gaze away, fixing it on a middle-aged swimmer churning up whitecaps in the lap lane. "If you want, you could also come over after class tomorrow, and I could shampoo your hair and then give you a few pointers with the styling brush and blow-dryer."

"That would be great!" Sailor beamed him a thankful smile. Then her shoulders sagged. "Except the Bards of Birkenstock committee meets every Tuesday. I have to get home and fix supper for my uncle before I head to the library."

"Wednesday then. Or Thursday. I'll make time for you whenever." *Just say the word.*

Her eyes sparkled as if he'd just offered her the Hope Diamond. "I have an extralong lunch break on Wednesdays. Would sometime between twelve and two work for you?"

Parker did a mental recap of his Wednesday schedule. He could probably shift his insurance agent's haircut and mustache trim a half hour earlier. Sandra, the makeup consultant, had asked him to touch up her highlights, but she wouldn't mind waiting another day or two.

Anticipation fizzed beneath his rib cage. "Come at twelve. I'll order takeout for us, and afterward I'll show you some styling tricks. What sounds good for lunch?"

"I can't let you do that."

"My pleasure. We both have to eat, don't we?"

Sailor chewed her lip. "At least let me bring lunch. How does salads from Audra's Café sound?"

"Make mine the Tuscan grilled chicken, extra meat, and you've got a deal."

❧

Sailor noticed Parker's new navy pin-striped trunks the moment he walked in the door for their Tuesday class. When she complimented him, he struck a male model's pose, swim towel slung over one shoulder. His quirky grin and wink turned her insides to gelatin. She spun around and dropped into the pool before the rest of the class could notice the blush warming her face.

After the class ended, another ten laps of full-out freestyle barely made a dent in her nervous energy. What was it about Parker Travis that so distracted her? Chandler Michaels arrived in town tomorrow! She needed to keep her eye on the goal and her mind off the unnervingly endearing hairstylist.

Later, at the Bards of Birkenstock meeting, Sailor presented the list of ideas she'd put together for Chandler's extended visit:

speaking at a high school assembly, holding a series of readings at the library, giving talks at local business clubs' weekly meetings, sitting in on book discussion groups, and of course all the requisite book-signing events.

"Wonderful ideas, Sailor." Donna DuPont jotted notes on her legal pad. "I'll let you take care of handling all the arrangements."

Great. She should have known.

Kathy patted her arm. "Don't worry, I'll help you make the calls."

Allan Biltmore leaned toward Sailor with a concerned frown. "Before you confirm too many of those engagements, let me run the list by Charles—excuse me, *Chandler*. We wouldn't want to overwhelm him."

Donna nodded. "Good point. Would you give us an update on Friday's dinner plans, Allan?"

"It's shaping up to be a delightful evening. Chandler wants things relaxed and homey, so the attire is dressy casual. For the menu, he reminded me his favorite meal growing up was something his Polish grandmother made called *bigos*, or hunter's stew. Nelda, my wife, has been scouring the Internet for recipes. I understand it's very meaty, with bacon, sauerkraut, and spices."

Sailor's stomach lurched. Maybe she should fill up on veggies before the dinner and hope no one noticed if she only took a few bites.

"I'd like a really good turnout," Allan continued, "so feel free to bring a family member or friend. Just let me know by noon Thursday so we know how many to prepare for."

On the way to the parking lot after the meeting, Kathy stopped by Sailor's car. "Think you'll invite anyone to go with you to Chandler's dinner?"

"Me? No." Sailor juggled her folder of meeting notes and poked around the side pocket of her purse for her car keys. "You're my best friend, and you'll already be there. And poor

Uncle Ed would be completely adrift at a function like that."

Kathy rested a hip against the fender and crossed her ankles. "I wasn't talking about your uncle. I thought maybe. . ." She wiggled her eyebrows. "Parker Travis?"

Sailor's keys slipped from her grasp and clattered to the pavement. When she stooped to retrieve them, her folder splayed open, and a gust of wind sent her notes skittering between the parked cars. "Great, just great."

She chased papers in one direction while Kathy scurried in another. With most of the pages corralled and back in the folder, Sailor unlocked the car and shoved everything across to the passenger seat. Huffing, she straightened to face Kathy. "Thanks for helping. Sorry I snapped at you."

Kathy folded her arms around her zippered portfolio. "I didn't realize mentioning Parker's name would throw you into such a tizzy."

"It didn't. I—" Sailor inhaled a calming breath before her pitch rose any higher. "I can't imagine what made you think I'd even consider asking Parker."

"Well, I know you've been seeing more of each other lately."

"He's in my class, and he did my hair. I wouldn't exactly call that *seeing* each other." Why Sailor felt she had to be so defensive, she had no clue. She dropped into the driver's seat and stabbed her keys into the ignition.

Kathy leaned over the top of Sailor's open door. "Then maybe I'll invite him. I wouldn't mind showing up with a handsome guy on my arm."

Sailor's fingers tightened around the steering wheel. "I didn't know you knew Parker that well."

"We had a nice chat at the library the other day and found out we have some. . .common interests."

"That's great. Then you should invite him." Sailor forced a tight-lipped smile and reached for the door handle. "It's getting late. Uncle Ed will worry."

Kathy waved good-bye as Sailor backed out of her parking

space. Something about her friend's self-satisfied smile evoked a twinge of suspicion.

Then it dawned on her that Kathy hadn't once lectured her this evening about her crush on Chandler Michaels. In fact, she'd hardly even alluded to it in almost a week. If Kathy's budding interest in Parker Travis diverted her from bad-mouthing Chandler, it would sure make life easier for Sailor.

eleven

"There you go, Pete. Good for another month." Parker swirled the black cape off his mustachioed insurance agent, strewing salt-and-pepper hair clippings across the floor.

"Fastest trim I ever got." Pete Walden collected his tan blazer from the coat hook. "If I didn't know better, I'd think you were rushing me out of here for a hot date."

Parker reached for the broom and dustpan. His sweeping motions hurried Pete out of the cubicle. "Carla will set up your next appointment. Good seeing you."

"I'm going, I'm going!" Pete looked skyward with a chuckle and strode toward the front. The last words Parker could make out were, "Must be one special lady."

Oh, she is, believe me. Not that he was happy about being so transparent. Everyone in the salon seemed to have picked up on his agitation this morning. Now, as he started rearranging tables in the break room and setting out the lime green picnic ware he'd borrowed from his mother, the rumors started flying big-time. By then there was no sense denying the obvious: He'd invited someone special to lunch.

He turned from adjusting the miniblinds over the back window to see Carla leaning in the doorway. A wide grin lit her face. "She's here. Shall I send her on back?"

Parker's stomach catapulted into his throat. Would he look too anxious if he hurried out front to meet Sailor? He'd have a hard enough time convincing her he regularly set out real plates and flatware for takeout.

He gulped. "Thanks, Carla. And maybe you and the others wouldn't mind eating at your stations today?"

"No prob." She winked an aqua-frosted eyelid. "Enjoy your lunch date."

While he waited, he tried a few nonchalant poses. First he leaned against the counter with his hands in his pockets. Nope, too bored looking. He grabbed a styling magazine off a bookshelf and plopped into a chair. Uh-uh, too disinterested. He tossed the magazine onto the shelf.

His nose twitched as the odor of burned coffee wafted his way. He glanced toward the other end of the counter and leaped to his feet. Someone had emptied the coffeepot without turning off the heating element.

"Terrific." He flicked the OFF switch and jerked the carafe off the burner. Without thinking he turned on the sink faucet and stuck the carafe under the flow. The shock of cold water hitting hot glass shattered the carafe instantly. Parker released the handle with a yelp.

Something hit the floor behind him a split second before Sailor appeared at his side. "What happened? Are you hurt?"

"I don't think so—" Then he saw the blood seeping from his left palm. Pain sliced up his arm.

"Here, hold it under the water." Sailor guided his hand beneath the tap, and he sucked in his breath as the stream washed over the wound. Red swirls circled the white porcelain sink and slid down the drain.

Sailor tore several paper towels from the dispenser. When the flow of blood diminished, she turned off the water and wrapped the towels around his hand. "It looked a lot worse at first, but I don't think it's deep. Come sit down, okay? And keep pressure on it."

Rewind, rewind. Not exactly the way Parker had envisioned their lunch date starting out. How could he have been so stupid? He caught sight of the Audra's Café take-out bag where Sailor had dropped it near the door. "Nothing like a little blood to ruin your appetite, huh?"

She followed his gaze. "Don't worry about it. Here, let me see if your hand has stopped bleeding." With gentle fingers she peeled aside the paper towels.

His palm looked pink and puckered from the cold water, but only the slightest traces of red oozed from the cut. He blew through pursed lips. "Whew. I think I'm gonna live."

"Oh please. It's hardly a scratch." Sailor gave an exaggerated shudder and strode to the sink. "What were you trying to do here anyway?"

"Someone left an empty coffeepot on the burner." Parker dabbed at his cut, now barely visible. Embarrassment aside, he'd been enjoying Sailor's TLC and was almost sorry the bleeding had been stanched so quickly.

"Don't tell me you stuck hot glass under cold water! That's incredibly dangerous." Sailor started opening drawers and cabinets. "Do you have any paper sacks around?"

He stood. "Leave it. I'll take care of it later."

"I don't mind." In the next cupboard she found a stack of paper grocery bags. She spread one open and set it on the floor then began extracting the larger pieces of glass and dropping them into the bag.

"Be careful. I don't want you getting cut." Parker nudged her aside and used the paper towel to finish clearing glass from the sink. He rinsed the smallest shards down the drain and turned to find Sailor carefully folding the top of the bag closed. "Let me take that out to the Dumpster, and you can open up those salads for us. There's bottled water and iced tea in the fridge."

When he returned from the alley, Sailor had dished their salads out of the plastic take-out containers and onto the picnic plates. She unscrewed the cap from a water bottle and poured it over the ice cubes in her glass. Looking up with a shy smile, she said, "I wasn't sure what you wanted to drink."

He grabbed an iced tea and sank into his chair. "Thanks for picking up lunch." With a grimace he added, "And no extra charge for the floor show."

Sailor spread an aqua-and-green-patterned napkin on her lap. "I don't know what I'd do if my new hairstylist were incapacitated. I'm counting on you for Friday night, you know."

He knew. All too well. "Shall I say grace?"

"Please." Sailor folded her hands on the edge of the table.

As he offered up thanks for the meal, Parker had trouble keeping his eyes lowered and his thoughts reverent. After the "amen," he tacked on a silent plea for the Lord's guidance in helping him protect Sailor from the lecherous Chuck Michalicek.

He picked up his knife and fork and tried to slice through the chicken breast without putting undue pressure on his cut. Maybe it was minuscule, but it stung like crazy. "What time is the dinner?"

"We're invited at six for mingling and appetizers, with dinner at seven. They're serving some kind of meat stew Chandler's grandmother always made. It sounds really artery clogging." She made a face and pushed aside a fried wonton. "Audra knows I don't eat these. Guess whoever filled the order didn't get the message."

One of the chapters in Chandler's guidebook dealt with how to get your date to share your interests. Parker decided he'd rather learn Sailor's likes and dislikes and show her he cared about her as a person. *Note to self: Sailor eats healthy.* "Your salad looks good. Is that salmon?"

"It's the Asian salad with grilled salmon and ginger dressing on the side—my absolute favorite."

"I'll have to try it sometime." He popped the cap off the small container of Italian dressing that came with his salad and drizzled it over the greens. "If you come in around four thirty for me to do your hair, will that give you time to change for dinner?"

"Four thirty should be fine." She sagged against the chair. "Except I have no idea what I'm going to wear. Mr. Biltmore said dressy casual. Casual for me is sweats over my bathing suit."

Parker didn't dare say out loud how fabulous she looked in a bathing suit. "We do have a wardrobe consultant here. I'd be happy to—"

"No, Parker, you're doing enough already. I'll see if Kathy

can go shopping with me after work tonight." She gave her head a sudden shake. "Scratch that. She has choir practice on Wednesday evenings. Maybe tomorrow. She'll probably want to find something cute to wear, too, since—" She drew her lip between her teeth and angled him a secretive look.

He laid down his fork. "What?"

"You'll find out soon enough."

Whatever it was, the warning pinch in his gut told him he wasn't going to like it.

❧

Back in her swimsuit, Sailor gazed at her reflection in the ladies' locker room mirror. What a shame she had to get in the pool again and ruin the perfect style Parker had helped her achieve. After lunch he'd given her another luxurious shampoo that turned her brain to languid mush beneath his fingers. Then he'd shown her step-by-step how to use a round styling brush to section off her hair and dry it into soft curves around her face. When they finished, he'd selected a few of the products he'd used from a display case in the reception area but once again refused to charge her for anything.

"Goodness, he's a nice guy." She turned from the mirror and checked the wall clock—nearly three. Allan Biltmore should be on his way home from the Springfield-Branson National Airport after picking up Chandler Michaels.

Sailor's stomach flip-flopped. Of all the days to be stuck teaching classes at the Y! The ladies from Willow Tree would be arriving any moment for their water aerobics class. Much as she loved them, she'd much rather be saying her first hellos to Chandler right about now—even though the very idea reduced her to a bundle of raw nerves. With a frustrated groan she pulled on a pair of sweats and hurried to the lobby.

The Willow Tree passenger van had just pulled up in front of the sliding glass doors. Donning her competent instructor facade, Sailor joined the driver at the rear of the van to retrieve a couple of walkers and a folding wheelchair then helped the ladies out the side door.

"Oh Sailor, I love your new haircut!" The white-haired Mrs. Parker plopped into the wheelchair. "You've been to see my grandson, haven't you?"

Sailor sucked in a breath. "Parker Travis is *your* grandson? He mentioned his grandmother took my classes, but I hadn't put two and two together. Why didn't you say something before?"

Mrs. Parker waved a hand in front of her face. "Didn't want to come across as a meddling old granny."

"You, meddling?" Sailor laughed and gripped the wheelchair handles. "The name Parker—I should have realized."

"My husband and I didn't have any sons, so Laura and our son-in-law named their boy Parker to pass along the family name."

"It's a nice name—although confusing at first." Sailor steered the chair through the double doors into the pool area.

"I'm so glad you and my grandson are getting acquainted. His mother and I have been waiting a long, long time for him to meet a nice young lady like you."

Sailor's cheeks tingled. She halted the wheelchair near the pool steps and locked the brakes. "I may have to change my mind about that 'meddling' business."

The elderly woman chuckled and allowed Sailor to help her out of the zip-up terry robe covering her skirted blue swim-suit. "I suppose by now you've figured out who gave you the tickets to the Frankie Verona show."

"That was. . .very nice of you." *And why am I not surprised?* Sailor bit her tongue to keep from saying how she really felt about such manipulative tactics while she aided Mrs. Parker's cautious descent into the pool.

A few of the more mobile ladies were already splashing around doing their warm-up exercises. Buoyed by the water, the arthritic Mrs. Parker moved with a freedom she could never enjoy on dry land—a sight that warmed Sailor's heart even as she mentally chided the woman for her misguided attempts at matchmaking.

❧

On Thursday evening Parker followed Grams's wheelchair down the long corridor to her apartment and held the door as she rolled inside. "Thanks for inviting me for supper," he said. "The Willow Tree buffet sure beats the frozen Szechuan chicken I was planning to heat up in the microwave."

"You're welcome to join me anytime." Grams allowed Parker to help her into her favorite chair and then reached for the pull chain on the nearby table lamp. "Want to start some decaf? My friend Margaret brought me a loaf of zucchini bread yesterday."

"Sounds good." Parker flipped the light switch in the kitchenette and found a package of french vanilla decaf in the freezer. "One cup or two?"

"Just one for me. Tell me more about this dinner party you're going to. The Biltmores are hosting, you said? That old goat's been around almost as long as I have."

He should have known once he mentioned the Chandler Michaels dinner engagement that he'd never hear the end of it from Grams. "Mr. Biltmore may be getting up in years, but apparently he's very active with the Birkenstock Arts and Letters Association."

Grams gave a cynical laugh. "Unless my memory's getting as unreliable as my joints, literature was never your best subject. How'd you end up on your former English teacher's guest list?"

"A friend on the committee invited me. Kathy Richmond, the librarian." Kathy's call last night had thrown him for a loop, but he couldn't refuse a chance to size up Chuck Michalicek in person. *And* keep an eye on Sailor. He filled the water reservoir and turned on the coffeemaker. "Want your zucchini bread warmed up?"

"With a dollop of butter, please. I heard our sweet little Sailor Kern is on the Bards of Birkenstock committee. She'll be there, I'm sure."

"Probably so." He found the zucchini bread wrapped in foil in the refrigerator. Finding a cutting board, he sliced off two good-sized slabs, spread them with butter, and set the plate in the microwave. The coffeemaker beeped the ready signal a few minutes later, and he served their dessert and coffee in Grams's cozy sitting room.

Parker slid a forkful of zucchini bread between his teeth and let the moist, buttery sweetness dissolve on his tongue. "Mmm, good stuff."

Grams blew across her coffee and took a careful sip. "*Probably* so?"

He shot his grandmother a confused look. "Probably so, what?"

"You said Sailor would *probably* be at the Biltmores'. Come now, Parker. You're not fooling anyone." She set down her mug and dabbed her lips with a pink paper napkin. "There's only one reason you'd ever be caught dead at a fancy dinner party, much less a *literary* dinner party, and that's because *she's* going to be there. You're smitten, and there's no use denying it."

Parker slid his dessert plate onto the low table in front of him. He scraped his palms up and down his temples. "Maybe I am. But *she's* smitten with Chandler Michaels."

"Does she know he's really Charles Michalicek? Does she know how that man hurt your aunt Ruthy, not to mention countless other young women blinded by his charms?"

"Yes to the first question, no to the second. And that's what scares me to death."

❧

Uncle Ed flaked off a bite of the pecan-crusted tilapia Sailor had prepared for their supper. "Sissy food, that's what this is. Your aunt Trina knew how to fry up a tasty batch of catfish."

Sailor stabbed a forkful of green beans. "I'd be happy to *grill* you some catfish sometime."

"Not the same. Not the same at all."

It wouldn't do any good to remind him how pleased his

doctor was when his latest cholesterol reading dropped fifteen points from last time. Uncle Ed seemed happiest when he had something to complain about, and Sailor's cooking was as safe a target as any.

Finishing her meal, she carried her dishes to the sink. "Kathy's picking me up in a few minutes to go shopping. Anything you need?"

"Can't think of a thing. Can't think what you need to go spending your hard-earned money on either."

Sailor capped the salad dressing and set it in the refrigerator. "I told you, I need something nice to wear to the dinner at Allan Biltmore's tomorrow night."

"Oh, right, for that loony tunes romance writer." Uncle Ed poked at a cherry tomato on his salad plate and flinched when the juice squirted him in the eye. "Do your parents know how you're spending your evenings?"

Guilt niggled Sailor's nape. No doubt her parents would have a few things to say about her infatuation with Chandler Michaels—exactly why she purposely kept her e-mails vague when describing her involvement with the Bards of Birkenstock committee.

The sound of a car horn saved her from coming up with a reply to her uncle's question. "There's vanilla pudding in the fridge for your dessert. I'll be home before ten."

Scooping up her purse, she fled out the front door and plopped into the passenger seat of Kathy's car. "Let's shop till we drop!"

Kathy threw the gearshift into REVERSE. "This has got to be a first—Sailor Kern excited about a shopping excursion."

"I've never had a reason to care before. But tomorrow night—"

"I know, I know. Tomorrow night you get to meet the romance writer of your dreams." Kathy turned at the next corner and aimed her car toward downtown.

"I can hardly believe he's here already." Sailor's feet did a happy dance on the floorboard. She felt sixteen again—or at least how sixteen *should* have felt. "We probably shouldn't drive by the Biltmores' to see if we could catch a glimpse of him."

Kathy angled her a look. "Probably not."

Birkenstock's shopping district wasn't huge, so it didn't take long for Sailor and Kathy to investigate the ladies' apparel offerings. If Kathy hadn't been along, Sailor might have settled for the first long-sleeved, calf-length basic black dress she laid eyes on in Mabry's Department Store.

"Give me a break, Sailor. You're going to a party, not a funeral." Kathy steered her to a rack of tops and slacks in bright spring colors. "This peasant blouse is *you*. And the swirls of aqua will bring out your eyes."

Sailor squinted and held a hand to her brow. "I've never worn anything that colorful in my life."

"And it's about time. Go try it on with these white cropped pants."

"For a dinner party?" Sailor frowned and tried to shove the garments back on the rack. Despite her intentions to choose something stylish and tastefully alluring, she found it wasn't as easy as she'd hoped to take this next step out of her comfort zone. "I thought maybe a nice skirt. . . ."

"Trust me. A cute necklace and earrings, maybe some white canvas espadrilles, and you'll be the belle of the ball." Kathy herded Sailor toward the dressing room. "And I expect you to model for me. I'll be checking out those silk blouses."

In the privacy of the dressing room, Sailor held up the pants and top and cast a doubtful gaze at her reflection. Quite a change from the usual conservative styles in humdrum colors that comprised the bulk of her wardrobe.

But where had conservative and humdrum gotten her? Absolutely nowhere.

"And where, exactly, do you want to be?"

The thought took her by surprise—a voice soothingly familiar and yet one she hadn't been paying much attention to lately. Her throat tightened. She sank onto the narrow bench beneath a chrome hook. Where *did* she want to be?

Not so much where, as with whom. She wanted to be with someone who saw her perfectly and loved her unconditionally, just like those couples in the romance novels. Someone who cared what she thought, who listened when she spoke, who looked at her as if no one else mattered in the world.

"And you think Chandler Michaels is that someone?"

Only a man who knew how to touch a woman's heart could write stories like those. Before the voices of doubt grew any louder, she slipped out of her jeans and into the chic new outfit she hoped would magically transform her into the woman Chandler Michaels would want to spend the rest of his life with.

twelve

Parker straightened the combs and brushes lining his styling-tools drawer then did the same with an array of gels, mousses, and hair sprays on the shelf opposite the mirror. He checked his watch—4:27. He'd rushed his last two afternoon appointments through so there'd be no chance of running over into the time he'd set aside for Sailor.

His visit with Grams last night had left him only slightly more hopeful about his chances with Sailor. After he'd explained the idea Kathy Richmond had come up with—using Chandler's romance book as the perfect guide to how *not* to romance a woman—Grams had reminded Parker he already owned the best romance guidebook ever written: the Holy Bible itself, God's love letter to His children.

"And if you *really* want to get down to pure romance," Grams had said, "just turn to the Song of Songs. Never were more romantic words penned than Solomon's poems about his beautiful lover."

Home in his apartment last night, he'd opened his Bible to the Song of Songs. The elegant poetry in simile and metaphor carried him places in his heart he'd never allowed himself to imagine. To love someone so purely, so deeply, so openly, so reverently—to experience a love that so beautifully mirrored God's own love for His children—Parker's longing to personally experience such love became a gnawing hunger.

And he felt more certain than ever that he wanted it with Sailor Kern.

"Hi, Parker."

At the sound of her voice, the can of hair spray he'd been holding clattered to the tile floor. He sucked in a breath and forced a grin. "Hey, right on time."

Sailor glanced at the hair spray can rolling around between their feet. "Good thing that wasn't glass."

"No kidding." If he needed any further convincing of his total head over heels attraction to Sailor, his terminal klutziness in her presence ought to be plenty.

Time to focus, Parker. She expected him to be the consummate professional, and that's what he had to be. . .for now.

&

By the time she left the shop, Sailor once again felt like Cinderella transformed. Pamela had touched up her manicure, Sandra had done her makeup, and Parker had styled her hair in a glamorous side-swept 'do that would show off the aqua hoop earrings Kathy had urged her to buy to match her outfit.

At home she slipped quietly in the back door. No way Uncle Ed could miss the changes in her appearance this time.

"That you, Sailor?" he called from the living room.

"I only have a few minutes to change for the dinner party." She scurried down the hall to her bedroom.

Closing the door, she took a few slow breaths. She had nothing to feel guilty about. She was an adult, after all, a red-blooded, passionate, thirty-two-year-old woman. A woman who was tired of looking mousy or—even worse—invisible. A woman who was ready to break out of her shell and start living.

She'd showered before leaving the Y, so all she had to do was slip into her new clothes. Careful not to muss her hair or manicure, she changed into the white crop pants and aqua-print blouse. The flowing fabric draped across her shoulders in a flattering line, with a self-tie that cinched her waist. Translucent sleeves angled to a point below her elbows. When she added the beaded necklace and bracelet, hoop earrings, and the white espadrilles, she stood before the mirror and gasped at the attractive woman gazing back at her.

At a few minutes after six she slipped down the hall and out through the kitchen before Uncle Ed could catch a glimpse of her. Any criticism from him would mar the wonderful evening she'd been dreaming of ever since she learned of Chandler's early return to Birkenstock.

"I'm leaving, Uncle Ed," she called from the back door. "Last night's leftovers are in the fridge. You can warm them up when you're ready."

"You mind your manners at that party, young lady. Remember who you are."

"Yes, sir." How many times had she been issued that warning? "Remember who you are" actually meant "Remember who your uncle and parents are, and don't embarrass or shame us."

She had no intention of doing either. She only wanted to be seen and loved for who she truly was, not as some goody-two-shoes phony.

Ten minutes later she arrived at the Biltmores'. Cars already lined the street, and she had to park three houses down from the posh brick two-story. She didn't see Kathy's car yet—but then Parker might be driving. The thought of them together caused a tiny pinch under her rib cage, which she quickly shook off as she marched up the sidewalk. Chandler Michaels, the man of her dreams, waited somewhere beyond the Biltmores' beveled-glass front door.

She reached for the bell with nervous fingers while her other hand clamped down on the new white woven clutch that matched her shoes. *Get a grip, Sailor. This is the moment you've been waiting for.*

Allan Biltmore greeted her with a gallant smile. "Welcome, Sailor! Come in, come in." He looked beyond her shoulder. "What, no date? I thought sure a young lady as lovely as you—"

"Nope, I'm by myself." With a steadying breath she marshaled what confidence she could and strode into the marble-tiled entry hall.

"I'm sure you're anxious to meet our guest of honor. He's in the living room."

Sailor's heart stammered out an erratic staccato as she followed

Allan Biltmore through a broad archway. In the living room a gaggle of committee members and guests surrounded someone seated near the fireplace. The way everyone oohed and aahed and generally fawned over everything the person said, it could only be Chandler.

Allan took Sailor's elbow and pushed forward through the group of admirers. "Here she is, Chandler, the young lady who's arranging your personal appearances during your stay. May I introduce Sailor Kern."

The crowd parted, and Allan stepped aside. Sailor's eager gaze fell upon a complete stranger—a stoop-shouldered, gray-haired man who looked nothing like the book jacket photo she'd been swooning over.

The man extended a shaky hand. "Nice to meet you, Miss Kern. Call me Chandler or Charles or Chuck—whichever you prefer. I'll answer to just about anything these days."

A hiccup of a breath caught in her throat. She blinked and stared at his outstretched hand then looked into his face again— a nice enough face, a smile she realized wasn't entirely unfamiliar, eyes that carried a hint of sadness. Her gaze slid downward, now taking in the wheelchair in which he sat—and Allan's mention of Chandler's "special requirements" took on a new meaning. She'd been imagining things like chauffeuring, secretarial help, more of those unfamiliar Polish menu preferences.

Something was wrong with this picture—very, very wrong.

❧

Kathy squeezed Parker's arm. "Do you see Sailor anywhere? I know she's here. I saw her car down the street."

"Not so far—wait, that's her over by the fireplace." A blaze ignited in Parker's chest. "Wow!"

"I'll say. Love what you did with her hair. She looks like a model."

An appreciative sigh slid between Parker's lips. "Definitely the prettiest girl here."

Kathy elbowed him in the ribs. "Hey, buster, *I'm* your date tonight, remember."

A server paused before them with a tray of hors d'oeuvres. Kathy took a napkin and helped herself, but Parker's stomach was already in knots—for more reasons than he cared to count. Seeing Sailor looking so gorgeous, confronting Chuck Michalicek, wishing he didn't have to pretend to be Kathy's date. . .

"Who's the guy Sailor's talking to?"

Parker followed Kathy's gaze. "The guy in the wheelchair? I don't—" An invisible fist slammed him in the solar plexus. "I think it's Chuck."

Kathy gasped. "*That's* Chandler Michaels?"

Before Parker could react, Allan Biltmore stepped in front of them. "Good evening, Kathy. And Parker, how nice you could join us. Do come over and say hello to our guest of honor."

While Allan made the introductions, Parker shared a glance with Sailor, who smiled up at him with deer-in-the-headlights surprise. Clearly this wasn't the Chandler Michaels she—or any of them—had been expecting.

"Parker Travis. You were just a kid the last time I saw you." Chuck offered a trembling hand.

Reluctantly Parker accepted the handshake, weak but sincere. "How are you, Chuck?" Immediately his face burned at the inanity of the question. The guy was in a wheelchair, for crying out loud.

"I was just explaining to my new friend Sailor why I don't exactly look like my book jacket photo. It was taken several years ago, before I was diagnosed with multiple sclerosis."

"I—I'm sorry." Parker gave an awkward shrug and stuffed his hands into his pockets. He was truly sorry Chuck had multiple sclerosis, but it didn't change the past. And would this vulnerable version of Chandler Michaels leave Sailor even more susceptible to his charms?

"The prognosis isn't great, but I'm learning to make the best of things." Chuck extended one arm in a gesture that took in the roomful of dinner guests. "It's just so good to be home again."

"And we're all very proud of you, Charles." Allan Biltmore stepped beside Chuck. "I see my wife signaling that dinner is served. Shall we, everyone?"

Sailor fell in alongside Chuck's motorized wheelchair, already fawning over him as Parker feared she might. All he could do was continue the pretense of escorting Kathy as they merged into the buffet line.

"Well, that was quite a stunner." Kathy picked up a plate and served herself a small helping of thick, meaty stew from a stainless, gold-accented chafing dish. "He sure doesn't seem like the playboy type."

"Maybe not, but he sure has Sailor's sympathies." Parker watched Sailor carry her own and Chuck's plates out to the patio.

He and Kathy found seats in the living room, and he remembered all over again why he avoided such gatherings. Balancing a plate of food on his lap, avoiding kicking over the glass of tea by his feet, making sure not to dribble gravy down his shirt—definitely *not* his favorite form of socializing.

Halfway through the meal, he looked up to see Sailor crossing the room, a mug of something hot and steamy clutched between her hands. The evening breeze had tugged loose a few strands of her hair, but she still looked fabulous.

Kathy made room on the sofa for her. "You look like an icicle, Sailor."

She scooted in close to Kathy and shivered. "Chandler asked if we could eat outside. With the MS, he doesn't function as well when he gets too hot. Then the sun went behind the trees and the breeze picked up, and I told him I was sorry but I needed to warm up." She leaned forward. "Oh, and Parker, he asked if you'd come out and talk awhile."

"Me?" Parker grabbed his plate before it slid sideways off his knees.

Kathy nudged him. "Yeah, here's your chance to hobnob with a celebrity."

Celebrity or not, maybe it was time to clear the air with ol' Chuck. Parker deposited his plate on the kitchen counter and filled a mug with coffee before finding his way outside.

"Good, you got my message." Chuck directed Parker to the empty patio chair next to him.

"I thought you'd be surrounded by admiring fans. Where's your entourage?"

Chuck gave a helpless laugh. "They all deserted me after the sun went down."

"Sailor mentioned you don't handle heat well." Thankful he hadn't removed his tan blazer, Parker sipped his coffee.

"I've had a lot of adjustments to make as a result of my illness." Chuck angled his wheelchair toward Parker. "Until now I've worked hard to hide my condition. Several months ago, when I could no longer get around without the wheelchair, I ceased all public appearances. Then Donna DuPont contacted me about the Bards of Birkenstock award, and—"

"And you couldn't pass up the chance to let the hometown folks see what a raging success you've become." Parker didn't intend to sound so cynical, but he couldn't help himself.

Chuck closed his eyes briefly. "I—I came home hoping to redeem myself in the eyes of the people who knew me way back when. I hope you know how sorry I am for the pain I caused your family."

Parker stiffened. "I'm not the one who's owed an apology."

"I've already asked Ruthy for forgiveness, which she has very graciously given."

"You've been in touch with my aunt?"

"Years ago." Chuck folded his hands. "When I first got the diagnosis, I was a wreck. It seemed like the end of my career, the end of my life, the end of everything that mattered. I started to wonder if it was God's punishment for all the people—all the women—I'd hurt over the years."

Parker huffed. "I may not like you much, but I can tell you right now, that's not the way God works."

"Even so, I felt an urgency to make amends, and I knew I'd hurt Ruthy worst of all. Receiving her forgiveness made me even hungrier to know God. It may sound corny to say my illness helped me find Jesus, but it did. I'm not the same man I was when I left Birkenstock."

A tiny crack split the shell of Parker's resentment—but just for a moment, just long enough for him to recall the chapter he'd read last night in *Romance by the Book*: "How to Play the Field without Getting Caught."

He plopped his coffee mug onto the glass table and scooted to the edge of his chair. "If you really know Jesus, maybe you can explain to me how you could write—"

Across the patio, the french doors burst open and Allan Biltmore strode out. "There you are, Charles. I've opened a window in the living room, so you should be comfortable inside now. Do come in, and enjoy dessert and coffee with the other guests."

Chuck cast Parker a regretful glance and allowed Allan to help him over the sill and through the door. Coffee mug in hand, Parker stood on the threshold and watched as several guests quickly surrounded the esteemed Chandler Michaels.

And Sailor was right in the middle of them.

thirteen

Hair still damp from her Saturday-morning swim class, Sailor tapped on the YMCA director's open door. "Mrs. Slaughter, can I talk to you a minute?"

The slim woman looked up from her computer. "What can I do for you, Sailor?"

"I wanted to ask about lightening my schedule for the next few weeks." After the initial shock had worn off and she talked more with Chandler last night, she realized how necessary her assistance would be. Her romantic illusions might be shattered, but even with his physical limitations, Chandler couldn't be more charming.

Mrs. Slaughter toyed with a ballpoint. "You know you've become practically indispensable around here. Who'll cover your classes?"

"Josh offered to fill in with the swimming lessons, and Gloria said she could take over some of my office work. I'd still come in to teach my water aerobics classes."

"As long as it's only temporary." Mrs. Slaughter swiveled toward her computer screen and then shot Sailor a wink. "I just better not lose you to that hotsy-totsy romance writer."

Her face steaming, Sailor thanked the director and fled from the office.

She showered and changed then headed straight over to the Biltmores', where she and Chandler planned to have lunch and discuss the agenda for his stay. When his first request was to accompany her to a Sunday worship service, she asked what church he'd attended before he left Birkenstock.

"I. . .didn't," he answered with a sheepish frown. "Where do you worship, Sailor?"

She stabbed a chunk of chicken salad. "I've belonged to Mission Hills Bible Church practically my whole life. But lately worship seems—I don't know—not as fresh and alive to me. Last Sunday I visited Rejoice Fellowship, and I really liked it."

"Then let's go there."

It had been hard enough keeping her thoughts on God last Sunday after discovering Parker Travis played flute in Rejoice's praise band. Attending with Chandler Michaels? *Lord, help!*

Except now she could prove to Kathy once and for all that Chuck Michalicek had changed. This man seemed light-years removed from the womanizing prankster Josh Fanning had described and nothing like the shallow literary snob Kathy predicted.

At church on Sunday he sang and prayed with a fervor that raised goose bumps on Sailor's arms. There was nothing phony about his show of faith, and she longed to be kindled with that same spiritual fire. Throughout the days ahead, as she escorted him to service club meetings, book club discussions, and library readings, he talked more with her about how his faith had changed him, how the Lord had brought comfort and assurance as he dealt with the debilitating aspects of multiple sclerosis. Upon reflection Sailor realized even his most recent novels carried a subtle faith message. . .perhaps accounting for some of the gentle nudges toward God she'd been sensing lately.

Still, it tore at her heart to see the way he struggled to hold a knife and fork steady to eat a meal—not to mention the painstaking effort to scrawl his signature across the title page of one of his novels for an excited fan.

On their way to the Biltmores' following the Thursday-noon Lions Club meeting, Sailor marshaled her courage to suggest an idea that had been nagging at her all week. "Have you ever tried water aerobics?"

"Haven't been much of a swimmer since my days on the Birkenstock High School swim team." Chandler gave a low chuckle. "You mentioned your friendship with Josh Fanning. I'm sure he's told you I got booted for disciplinary problems."

"He. . .mentioned an incident." Sailor steered the rented handicap-accessible van into the Biltmores' circular driveway, where she'd left her car. "It's just that I was thinking how much more freely you could move in the water. I've read it could be good therapy for MS."

"Doing your homework, eh?"

"Isn't it worth a try if it could help?" She hurried around to the side door, released the safety latches on Chandler's wheelchair, and extended the ramp. "I'm teaching classes at the Y this afternoon. Why don't you come with me?"

"Sounds like fun, but I'm exhausted." Chandler steered his chair down the ramp. "If I don't catch up on some rest this afternoon, I'll be a zombie for the Methodist ladies' book club tomorrow morning."

"Maybe another time then."

Mrs. Biltmore met them at the door, and Sailor said goodbye and went to her car. She'd just pulled into the YMCA parking lot when her cell phone rang. She answered it on the way into the building.

"Hi, Kathy, what's up?"

"I was about to ask you the same question. We've hardly talked all week. Is Chuck keeping you that busy?"

"*Chandler* has had engagements every day and most evenings." She waved at Gloria on her way to the ladies' locker room. "I hope Donna wasn't too miffed that I didn't make the Tuesday committee meeting, but Chandler had an appointment with the chamber of commerce board to talk about the parade plans."

"Right, he's going to be the grand marshal." Kathy's tone mellowed. "Have I told you how proud I am of you? I knew it would be a stretch, but you've gone far beyond the call of duty."

Warmth filled Sailor's chest. She hung her purse on a hook inside her locker and laid out her towel and swimsuit. "I'm having a wonderful time getting to know Chandler. He's amazing."

"Nothing like what any of us were expecting, huh?"

"Nothing like." Sailor sighed. "I hope you see now what a great person he is. He's thoughtful, wise, incredibly kind. I can talk to him about anything."

"That's great, Sailor. So. . .no more romantic infatuation?"

"I wish you'd quit saying things like that."

"Before you met Chuck in person, you *were* hoping for something more than mere friendship—don't deny it."

"I won't, but—" Sailor sank onto the narrow wooden bench in front of the locker bay. How could she explain to her best friend the confusing mix of elation and discouragement now filling her? Chandler made her feel so special—important, needed, appreciated. He seemed to truly care about her thoughts and opinions. And when he talked about God, his words brought warmth and light to the deep places of her heart. She could honestly say she was growing to love Chandler, love him as a friend and mentor and spiritual confidant.

Yet a part of her still yearned for something more, for the romantic love of a man who only had eyes for her.

"Sailor, are you there?"

She sniffed. "Sorry, Kath. I've got to get ready for my class. Call you later, okay?"

She flipped the phone shut and stuffed it into her purse before changing into her swimsuit. Then once more she sank onto the bench. Leaning forward, she covered her face with her hands.

Dear God, I'm really out of practice in the prayer department, and I'm sorry we've been so out of touch. Help me find my way back to You. Help me trust that You really are in control of my life—including the romantic parts.

She started to rise then quickly added, *Oh, and please help me not to be jealous of Kathy and Parker. I only want them both to be happy. Amen.*

For the second Sunday in a row, Parker looked out from the Rejoice Fellowship chancel to see Sailor escorting Chuck Michalicek up the aisle. She had a bounce in her step, a perky self-confidence he'd only witnessed when she taught her classes at the Y. He should be glad—for more reasons than simply because he no longer had to worry about her being swept away by the Chandler Michaels persona.

Except he couldn't stop thinking about that stupid book. After he and Chuck were interrupted at the Biltmores' dinner, he'd never had another chance to corner the guy and ask him what possessed him—a professed *Christian!*—to write that piece of chauvinistic drivel.

Maybe today, if he could peel Chuck away from Sailor long enough. After the closing song, he gave his flute a cursory swab, packed it into its case, and hurried out front. "Hi, Sailor, Chuck. Nice to see you back at Rejoice."

"Oh, hi, Parker. Loved the music today." Sailor's hair swung around her shoulders as she turned to face him.

His fingers tingled with the memory of touching those silky tresses. It was all he could do to keep his hands at his sides. "Chuck, I was hoping for another chance to talk. Do you have lunch plans?"

"Sorry, Parker, but as soon as Sailor returns me to the Biltmores', Allan is driving me to the airport."

Parker lifted a brow and tried to keep the hopefulness out of his voice. "You're leaving already?"

"No, we're picking up my stepson." An edgy look flickered across Chuck's face before he covered it with a crooked smile. "Quentin has been my writing assistant for a few years now. Don't know what I'd have done without him, especially after his mother—my wife—passed away two years ago."

"I'm sorry. I didn't know you'd ever married." Parker stuffed his hands into his pockets.

"Irene was a nurse I met during one of my hospital stays.

She gets most of the credit for turning my life around and leading me to Christ."

Sailor checked her watch. "We'd better get going, Chandler. It was good to see you again, Parker. Sorry I haven't been available for those extra coaching sessions I promised you. Maybe after. . ."

He shrugged and nodded. "See you Tuesday, though?"

"You bet." Sailor followed Chuck's wheelchair toward the exit, and they were soon swallowed up in the crowd.

"Hey, son." Mom touched Parker's arm. "Was that who I think it was?"

Parker grimaced. "In the flesh."

She made a tsk-tsk sound. "I should have told you a long time ago that he apologized to Ruthy."

"So you knew?"

"She was already married to your uncle Jim by then, and she didn't want anyone making a big deal of it. It was enough for her to know Chuck finally got his act together."

But had he? Parker still couldn't reconcile the repentant, soft-spoken man in the wheelchair with the cocky, self-serving author of *Romance by the Book*.

ॐ

As Sailor parked the minivan in the Biltmores' driveway, Allan hurried over to open her door. "You should come with us to the airport, dear. I thought we'd stop for lunch in Springfield before picking up Quentin."

Chandler cleared his throat. "I'm sure Sailor has more exciting plans for her Sunday afternoon than making an airport run."

"Actually, no." Sailor shot Chandler a teasing grin. "Unless you have a copy of your next book I could curl up with for the afternoon."

"It. . .could be awhile before another Chandler Michaels romance is released." He angled his gaze toward the floorboard.

"Join us, Sailor. I'm sure you're as anxious as we are to meet

Charles's stepson." Allan slid open the left rear door for his wife.

Mrs. Biltmore climbed in and settled into the rear seat. "Plenty of room. Come on back, Sailor."

"Well. . .if you're sure it's okay." Leaving the driver's seat for Allan, Sailor buckled in next to the silver-haired Mrs. Biltmore. While Allan rechecked the tie-downs on Chandler's wheelchair, Sailor made a quick call to Uncle Ed to let him know her plans.

On the drive to Springfield, Sailor couldn't help noticing how subdued Chandler seemed. He'd been so full of life and energy at church that morning—at least until Parker caught up with them. Maybe being reminded of his wife again had him down. . .or possibly whatever Parker had wanted to talk with him about. Sailor couldn't shake the feeling that there was some kind of history between Parker and the Chuck Michalicek of the past. Why couldn't Parker—and everyone else who knew Chandler before—see him as he was now?

Arriving in Springfield, Allan stopped for lunch at a steak house. Sailor and Chandler both ordered grilled chicken salads, but Chandler barely touched his. With the few bites he attempted, his hands shook so horribly that he almost couldn't get the fork to his mouth. Sailor ached to help him, but he'd already rebuffed Allan's offer; she feared more attention would only embarrass him. He finally gave up, saying he wasn't so hungry after all.

At the airport Allan parked in the short-term lot. "You're looking tired, Charles. Why don't you wait in the van?"

Chandler nodded and sighed. "Thanks, I think I will."

Mrs. Biltmore patted Sailor's arm. "I'll stay with Charles if you want to go in with Allan. They may need an extra hand with the luggage."

Sailor trotted to keep up with Allan's long strides on their way to the baggage-claim area. "Do you know what he looks like?"

"I've only seen a photograph, but Charles said we wouldn't

have any trouble recognizing him."

Passengers were already retrieving their luggage when Sailor and Allan arrived at the carousel. Sailor scanned the crowd and wondered how exactly she was supposed to recognize a man she'd never seen before—until her glance landed on the handsomest face she'd ever laid eyes on. He had Matt Damon's rakish haircut, Hugh Jackman's seductive smile, Matthew Mc-Conaughey's sensitive gaze—

A shriek sounded to Sailor's left. "Oh my goodness, you're *him*! I just *love* your novels, Mr. Michaels. I'm reading *Love's Sweet Song* right now." The woman thrust a book at the tall, grinning man. "Would you sign it for me? Make it 'to Cheryl, my most adoring fan.'"

Sailor watched in stunned shock as the man accepted the book and scrawled something on the cover page—*as if he were Chandler Michaels himself!*

And then she realized that's exactly who he looked like. The debonair man in the leather jacket and open-collar shirt could have stepped right out of Chandler's book-jacket photo. Her breath snagged. Her heart ker-thumped. The image she'd clung to all these years, the Chandler Michaels of her dreams, now stood close enough that she could reach out and touch him.

Allan squeezed Sailor's elbow. "I think we've found Quentin."

%

"I think we've got problems."

Parker held his cell phone to his ear and nudged the car door shut with his hip. "Kathy? What are you talking about?"

"Quentin Easley."

"Quentin *who*?" Impatience gnawed Parker's gut. His knees ached like he'd climbed Mount Everest, and his shoulder felt like a T. rex had taken a bite out of it. He'd just finished one of his busiest Wednesdays on record—six haircuts, two highlights, three full colors, and a perm—all for women who were dying to make a lasting impression on the famed Chandler Michaels. Going public with his real identity *and* his multiple sclerosis only seemed to endear him to his loyal Birkenstock fans even more.

If they only knew.

Kathy gave an exasperated huff. "Haven't you heard? Chuck's stepson. He came to town last Sunday, and he is major trouble."

Parker trudged up the stairs to his apartment and let himself inside. "I've got half an hour before I have to be at church for a band rehearsal that I'm too tired to go to, thanks to Chuck's untimely arrival. Tell me why I should be worried about Quentin what's-his-name."

"Because Quentin Easley is everything we were afraid Chandler Michaels would be. And Sailor is falling for him."

"You've got to be kidding." Parker flopped onto the sofa. Now he could add a screaming headache to his growing list of complaints.

"Quentin came with Sailor to the Bards of Birkenstock meeting last night. Everybody was expecting 'Chandler Michaels,' and they weren't disappointed. Seems Quentin has been standing in for his stepfather in public venues for months."

"Chuck said something at church Sunday about his stepson being his assistant."

"Assistant? More like his clone. Quentin claims he's here only for Chandler's sake and assured the committee he wouldn't be any added expense, but there's something about him that makes me very worried about Sailor."

Parker rubbed his eyes and struggled for perspective. "Give her some credit, will you? She's smart, sensible—"

"And extremely vulnerable. And Quentin really knows how to play on her affections."

"You've met him—what? One time? How do you know he's all that bad?"

"There's a big signing event tomorrow evening at Dale & Dean's Book Corner. Come with me, and judge for yourself."

Parker reluctantly agreed to go, but as he threw a sandwich

together for a quick meal before praise-band practice, he hoped Kathy was wrong. Sailor had seemed so vibrant yesterday—even more so than normal as she skillfully and confidently coached his water aerobics class. If this was the result of spending time with Chandler Michaels—the real one or this new Quentin Easley version—what right did Parker have to interfere?

Lord, I only want what's best for her. If it means stepping aside for another man, give me the strength to do it. But if You've chosen Sailor for me, then help me do whatever it takes to win her heart.

fourteen

Sailor scooped a spoonful of leftover couscous into a plastic container. As usual, Uncle Ed had turned up his nose at the healthy recipe she'd tried. "Can I leave you with the dishes? If I don't hurry, I'll be late for Chandler's book signing."

Uncle Ed poked around in the refrigerator and came out with a jar of peanut butter. "That book writer fella has you hoppin' faster than a toad on a hot sidewalk. You've been dressing to the nines and out gallivanting nearly every night for the past two weeks."

"A couple more weeks and it'll be over." And probably so would her chances for romance. Quentin Easley had swept her off her feet the moment he took her hand at the airport baggage claim. He was everything she'd expected the real Chandler Michaels to be and more.

She pulled into the parking lot in front of Dale & Dean's Book Corner only moments before the Biltmores arrived. Quentin hurried to help Chandler out of the van. He looked up when Sailor approached and shot her a megawatt smile. "Hey, gorgeous. I've been waiting all day to see you again."

Her heart did a tiny flutter dance. She straightened her shoulders and tried to concentrate on business. "I stopped by this morning to check on the arrangements. Dean ordered an ample supply of all your titles, Chandler, and Dale situated the signing table just like you asked."

"Thank you, Sailor." He reached for her hand and gave it a feeble squeeze.

She noted the fatigue lines creasing the corners of his eyes and again felt thankful Quentin had come along to help. His assistance at Monday's book discussion group then fielding reporters' questions at yesterday's mayor's breakfast seemed to take much of the pressure off Chandler.

Within a few minutes of seating Chandler at his table, Sailor looked toward the front of the bookstore to see a steady stream of customers, all heading for the display featuring Chandler's books. A couple of younger shoppers spotted Quentin and rushed over, mistaking him for Chandler and gushing like the fan at the airport.

"Oh, Mr. Michaels, will you sign my copy of *The Heart's True Song*?" A brunette with a pixie haircut hugged the book to her bosom. "It's my absolute favorite."

Sailor stepped forward, ready to direct them to the real Chandler Michaels, but Chandler caught her arm. "It's all right; let them think he's me."

"But Chandler—"

"Quentin's doing me a favor, actually. Let's face it; a guy in a wheelchair who can barely hold a pen is *not* the dashing romance writer they want signing their books."

She chewed her lip, torn between wanting Chandler to have the recognition he deserved and her growing admiration for Quentin. He must really love and respect Chandler to work so hard at sparing him unnecessary awkwardness about his condition.

A poster of *Love's Sweet Song* stood on an easel near the table. Sailor's glance fell to the inset at the bottom right corner, Chandler Michaels's publicity photo. Or was it Quentin? Honestly she couldn't tell. She sank onto the folding chair next to Chandler. "I know you're not really related, but it's amazing how much he looks like. . .well, like I'd always pictured you."

"He does resemble me—the younger me—and of course he plays up that fact for the fans." Chandler's mouth flattened. "You're attracted to him, aren't you?"

She ducked her head. "What girl wouldn't be?"

"Appearances aren't everything, Sailor."

"You must think I'm really shallow." Her lips quirked in an

embarrassed smile. "It's more than his looks. I've never met anyone so charming, so fascinating. He makes me feel. . ." She couldn't bring herself to say the word *beautiful*.

The autograph seekers quickly gathered, ending their conversation. Later, as the line thinned, a tall woman in a navy pantsuit approached the table. "Hi, Chandler. Goodness, it sure feels weird to call you that. I'm Gina Williams—but you knew me as Gina Young. We sat next to each other in Mr. Ochoa's algebra class."

Chandler offered a warm smile. "Gina, of course. Don't tell me our class valedictorian reads romance novels?"

"Are you kidding? I love your books—and they're even more special since I realized you're my old classmate! Will you sign my copy?"

"Happy to." Chandler fumbled with the pen, and Sailor reached over to help him find the title page. He took a couple of shivery breaths that gave her a moment of concern, and then he looked up and said, "Spell your name for me, please?"

"G-I-N-A." The woman gave an awkward laugh. "I'm surprised you have to ask, considering all those mash notes you used to pass to me when Mr. Ochoa's back was turned."

He shook his head as if clearing it. "Sorry, I meet so many people on these book tours."

"Understandable." Gina glanced toward Quentin, still chatting it up with Chandler's younger admirers. "That guy definitely knows how to work a crowd."

Sailor stood. "That's Chandler's assistant, Quentin Easley. He's been a tremendous help."

"I'm sure." Gina nodded toward the wheelchair. "I read your interview last week in the *Birkenstock Times*. I'm so sorry about the MS."

Chandler cleared his throat. "Sailor, would you mind getting me another bottle of water?"

She hesitated to leave Chandler alone at the table—he seemed a little unsteady this evening—but there was no one else around to ask. "Sure. Be right back."

Dale, the younger of the bookstore's co-owners, had just set out a tray of cookies in the lounge area when Sailor caught up with him and asked about the water. While Dale went to get another bottle, Sailor paced the long row of bookshelves, keeping one eye on Chandler and the other on the rear passageway from which Dale would emerge.

"There you are, beautiful."

She spun around, caught her new sling-back stiletto on a tear in the carpet, and fell headlong into Quentin's outstretched arms.

"Whoa, baby! I wasn't expecting such an enthusiastic greeting."

Extracting herself from his embrace, Sailor straightened her skirt and smoothed her hair. Heat singed her cheeks. Her pulse stammered. "I—I was just waiting for Dale. Chandler needed some water—"

"He's fine—visiting with another old flame from his high school days. Which works out perfectly for me. I've been waiting to catch you alone so I could give you something." He reached into the inner pocket of his blazer and withdrew a foil-wrapped box topped with a miniature silver bow.

"Quentin—"

He silenced her with a finger to her lips, his touch like red-hot metal. "Just open it. I can't wait to see your face."

Lightness filled her chest, an excitement she almost felt guilty for giving in to—her first gift from a—well, she couldn't exactly call Quentin a boyfriend, at least not yet. With trembling fingers she pried off the lid and lifted out a tiny velveteen drawstring bag. Quentin held the box while she loosened the strings and emptied the contents into her palm—a gold charm in the shape of a human hand with thumb, index finger, and pinky extended.

"It's sign language for 'I love you.'" Quentin moved closer. "It might be a little soon, but I saw it in the window of a jewelry shop yesterday, and I immediately thought of you. You're special, Sailor. You're someone I think I could actually say those words to someday."

Her heart hammered out a frightening rhythm as Quentin's face moved closer, hovering above hers. His lips parted. His eyelids lowered. If not for his hand circling around and pressing against her back, she might have swooned—just like the heroine in *Love's Eternal Melody*.

"Oh, Quentin. . ."

ॐ

"Aw, Sailor. . ." Defeat and rage and despair tied a tangled knot in Parker's belly. He and Kathy had arrived at the bookstore five minutes ago, and not finding Sailor with Chuck, they'd browsed the aisles until they spotted her—just in time to see Quentin hand her the little silver box.

Bile rose in Parker's throat when he glimpsed the sparkly little charm, a trinket straight out of *Romance by the Book*. He remembered it from the chapter on "What Women Want": *"More than anything, a woman wants to believe you love her, and nothing says love to a woman like jewelry. A pearl necklace, a pair of heart-shaped earrings, an I-love-you charm—if you play your cards right, you'll have her right where you want her without having to spring for that diamond ring."*

Kathy punched him in the arm. "Now do you believe me?"

He turned away before the inevitable kiss. He couldn't bear to watch. "I think I'm going to be sick."

"I'm going to extract Sailor from this little tête-à-tête before things get any steamier." Kathy started down the aisle.

Parker grabbed her wrist. "Don't. . .embarrass her, okay?"

Kathy's shoulders sagged. "I'll make up some excuse about needing to talk to her about committee stuff."

With a groan Parker turned his attention to Chuck, still signing autographs at a table draped with a scarlet cloth. Chuck's hand suddenly jerked, and the pen toppled from his grip and clattered to the floor. Mouthing an apology to the waiting fan, he rolled his wheelchair back and bent to find the pen.

Parker could see the frustration growing in Chuck's face. He hurried over. "Here, I've got it."

Chuck looked up with a grateful half-smile. "Thanks. Bad case of writer's cramp."

"Maybe you should take a break."

"Yes. My assistant's around here somewhere. . . ." A confused look wrinkled Chuck's forehead.

The customer tapped her book on the table. "What about my autograph?"

Dean from the bookstore stepped forward. "Folks, we're going to take a short intermission. We have coffee, juice, fruit, and cookies over in the lounge area. Please help yourselves."

While the bearded bookstore owner herded disgruntled fans away from the table, Parker guided Chuck over to a quiet area at the far end of the oak veneer checkout counter. "Are you okay? You look a little out of it."

"I'd forgotten how exhausting these events are." Chuck rubbed his eyes and then fixed Parker with a slowly clearing gaze. "Guess I should thank you for rescuing me."

Parker gave a huff. "I thought your stepson-slash-assistant was supposed to be helping you, not making time with your local PR person."

Chuck's eyes widened. "Quentin's with Sailor? Oh no. . ."

"Oh, *yes*. And worming his way into her innocent heart with guerilla romance tactics from *your* tacky little book."

Chuck grimaced. His Adam's apple made a painful-looking trail up and down his throat. "You know about the book?"

"My friendly neighborhood librarian—who happens to be Sailor's best friend—loaned me her advance copy." Parker ran his hands through his hair. "I don't get it, man. Since your return to Birkenstock, everyone, including you, had me convinced you're a changed man. I've even been told your romance novels are all sweetness and chivalry. What possessed you to write such a boatload of garbage and call it a romance guide?"

"I didn't." Chuck tipped his head and squeezed his eyes shut. "Quentin wrote it."

"Quentin? *He* wrote *Romance by the Book*?"

"It's a long story." Chuck let out a ragged sigh and explained how he'd at first been flattered when Quentin took such an avid interest in becoming his writing assistant. As the multiple sclerosis progressed, Quentin helped by doing research, taking dictation, and typing manuscript pages. When Chuck had bad days and wasn't up to writing at all, he sometimes allowed Quentin to try his hand at fleshing out the scenes.

"He really mastered my style, and he has genuine writing talent. Then last year at a book signing, someone thought he was me. It occurred to me that if I dropped out of sight for a while and then let him take over my public appearances, no one need ever know about the MS. Eventually, when the time comes that I can no longer write the books myself, he will carry on the Chandler Michaels name."

Parker smirked. "So he really is your clone."

"It seemed like the perfect solution to keep my faithful fans happy for many years to come. . .until Quentin came up with the idea for *Romance by the Book*."

"And you let him?"

"He wouldn't show me the draft, said he wanted to surprise me. I didn't see the actual contents until the page proofs arrived a few weeks ago—and wouldn't have seen them then except the editor accidentally e-mailed them to my address instead of Quentin's."

"But you're still letting it go to press."

"The legal steps to transfer my 'Chandler Michaels' identity to Quentin are already set in motion. If I stop publication now, I'm afraid it would mean public humiliation for both of us. So many people have read and loved my books. I can't let the Chandler Michaels name be tarnished with scandal."

Parker snorted. "I'm not sure having your name on the cover of that piece of trash is much better."

"There's always the hope readers will think it was written

tongue in cheek." Chuck's clenched jaw indicated he believed no such thing.

❧

"There you are, Chandler." Sailor stepped forward and twisted the cap off a water bottle. She hoped her makeup camouflaged the blush warming her face. How much had Kathy seen before practically ripping her out of Quentin's arms?

Chandler looked even more fatigued than when she'd left him at the signing table. He thanked her for the water and took a sip. "Where's Quentin?"

"Mingling with the customers. Several were getting impatient." Sailor cast a worried glance at Parker. "Is everything okay here?"

Parker stood. "I think Chuck's had about all the public exposure he can handle for one evening. You should get him home to the Biltmores' ASAP."

"I'm fine, really." Chandler set the water bottle on the end of the counter and steered himself toward the signing table. His hand slid off the control, and he muttered a curse.

Sailor rushed over. "You've been running around like crazy the past couple of weeks. People will understand. Quentin can cover for you."

He heaved a pained sigh and tugged his hand into his lap. "Silly me. With Quentin here, no one will even notice the old guy in the wheelchair is gone."

The tone of his voice chilled Sailor. "Don't talk like that, Chandler. Think of all the people who've come especially to see the man they remembered from before."

"Exactly." Chandler pounded his thigh. "They all wanted to gawk at poor old Chuck Michalicek, erstwhile troublemaker and class clown, now a crippled has-been."

"That's not true." Sailor knelt in front of the wheelchair and covered his fist with her hands. "Your books have touched so many hearts. Your stories have made people believe in the power of love."

His gaze found hers, and the hard lines around his mouth

softened into a tender smile. "Sailor, Sailor. Such an innocent, always ready to see the good in everyone."

Innocent? She was so tired of being seen as naive little Sailor Kern, the missionaries' kid. Tired of everyone thinking they had to protect her from the world. At least Quentin didn't treat her like a child. He made her feel beautiful, desirable, more womanly than any man ever had, except for. . .

She pushed to her feet, her glance shifting to where Parker stood next to Kathy. The meaningful looks passing between the two of them were unreadable. Probably they couldn't wait until they could make polite excuses and get away together. The thought left a sour taste in Sailor's mouth, and she mentally chided herself for her misplaced jealousy.

Allan Biltmore strode over, a stack of books balanced on one arm. He set them by the cash register and turned to Chandler. "For my three granddaughters. They'll love them. I won't ask you to sign them tonight, though."

Sailor stepped in front of Allan, keeping her voice low. "I think you should take Chandler home. He doesn't seem well."

Allan's bushy white eyebrows drew together. "I wondered earlier if he was having difficulty. I'll fetch Nelda, and we'll get him straight home. Would you mind dropping Quentin off later?"

"Of course—"

Parker shouldered his way up to the counter. "I'll be happy to give Quentin a lift. There's no reason for Sailor to stay."

She spun around, fresh indignation filling her. "Excuse me? I can't just leave. I'm the one who arranged this event."

Taking a half step back, Parker lowered his gaze. "I thought since Kathy's here. . .if you wanted to get home early. . ."

Kathy tucked her hand beneath Parker's arm in a possessive gesture that made Sailor's stomach twist. "Never mind, Sailor. We can see you've got everything under control. Tell Quentin good-bye for us, will you? Come on, Parker, you promised me a decaf latte at Logan's Bistro. And I'm dying for one of their blueberry scones."

Kathy hurried Parker out the door before Sailor could apologize for snapping at him. Good grief, her emotions were in knots lately. She turned to see Allan and his wife helping Chandler gather up his jacket and briefcase. Moments later they said their good-byes, leaving Sailor to close out the book signing with Quentin.

Older fans filtered out shortly after Chandler left, but the younger crowd remained enthralled by Quentin and didn't dissipate until nearly nine. Sailor's feet ached from standing so long in heels, and her cheek muscles felt frozen into a permanent smile. She could hardly wait to get home, kick off her shoes, and slip into her comfy cotton pajamas.

When the last customer headed out the door, Quentin whistled out a relieved sigh and draped his arm around Sailor. Pulling her close, he planted a kiss on her temple. "Thanks, babe. Couldn't have done it without you."

While Dale, Dean, and a couple of their clerks started clearing the table and straightening the book displays, Quentin helped Sailor on with her sweater. "How about you and I go somewhere quiet and relax for a while? It's been a long night."

"I shouldn't. Tomorrow's going to be another busy day." She tried to focus on anything but the flames Quentin's fingers ignited as he stroked her cheek. A bizarre mixture of anticipation and fear squeezed her heart. Hadn't she always dreamed of having a man treat her this way? Hadn't she always dreamed it would be Chandler Michaels. . .or at least the closest thing to him?

Thinking of Chandler, she stiffened. "Anyway, we should check on Chandler. He didn't look at all well when they left. I'm worried about him."

"That's what I love about you—always thinking of someone else." Quentin drew her under his arm and escorted her toward the exit. "Poor guy, the MS seems to get worse every day. I told him this trip wasn't such a good idea, but he insisted. I'll be surprised if he makes it to the festival."

fifteen

When Parker didn't see Sailor and Chandler in church the following Sunday, he hoped it only meant they were visiting elsewhere. On the other hand, it didn't surprise him in the least not to see them arrive with Quentin Easley in tow. Parker doubted the creep had ever so much as set foot inside a church.

After spending Monday morning doing the ladies' hair at the Willow Tree Assisted-Living Center then a busier-than-normal Tuesday at the salon, Parker was more than ready for his water aerobics class that afternoon.

As he prepared to blow-dry a client's hair, Carla buzzed him on the intercom. "Call on line 2. A lady from the Y."

Parker's nerves sang. *Sailor?* He snatched up the phone and tried to keep his voice level. "This is Parker."

An unfamiliar female voice responded. "Hi, it's Gloria from the Y. Sorry to call at the last minute, but Sailor had to cancel her classes this afternoon due to a personal emergency."

"I. . .see." Only he didn't. Nausea churned beneath his belt buckle. If Quentin Easley had anything to do with this—

"Sailor usually offers a makeup lesson whenever she has to cancel. I'm sure she'll be in touch. Plan on next week as usual unless you hear otherwise."

"Right. Thanks." He hung up and switched the hair dryer on, the whir masking his spinning thoughts.

Since he was free for the rest of the afternoon anyway, Parker left shortly after his last client. He headed straight for the library, hoping Kathy might know what was going on with Sailor.

"I don't know much." Kathy motioned him to the end of the checkout desk. "I heard Chuck had a rough weekend and

130

had to cancel most of his appearances."

"He wasn't looking good Thursday night, that's for sure." Parker absently jangled the coins in his pocket. "Have you talked to Sailor since then?"

"Briefly. She's very worried about Chuck. Apparently they've formed a real connection since he came to town."

Parker snorted. "Better him than his stepson. I don't trust that guy farther than I can throw him."

When another librarian approached their end of the desk with a stack of books, Kathy reached under the counter for her purse. "I'll be back in ten, Zoe."

She led Parker to the elevator, and they rode it downstairs to the snack bar. Seated at a corner table, Kathy pulled out her cell phone. "I'll call Sailor right now and find out what's going on."

"Don't mention I'm here. Might give her the wrong idea."

"What, that we're checking up on her?" Kathy flicked one hand at him while flipping open her cell phone with the other. "Oh, hi, Sailor. I didn't expect you'd actually answer. Isn't this your class time?"

Smooth. Very smooth. Parker leaned back and folded his arms while listening to Kathy's side of the conversation. It sounded as if Chuck had taken a serious turn for the worse and was returning to New York.

"That's awful, Sailor. Give him my best, will you? And call me when you get home from the airport." Kathy pressed the DISCONNECT button and shoved the phone into her purse.

Parker sat forward. "Chuck's leaving Birkenstock?"

"It's kind of a good-news/bad-news thing." Kathy ran a knuckle along her jaw. "The good news is Chuck's setback is treatable, but he wants to see his own doctor. They're on the way to Springfield right now so Quentin can fly him home."

"And the bad news?"

"Quentin's catching a return flight on Thursday so he can fill in at the rest of Chuck's scheduled appearances, including the book festival."

Parker pressed his thumbs into his eye sockets. "Without Chuck here to keep Sailor busy and deflect Quentin's overtures, she'll be an easier target than ever."

"Which means you need to step up your game plan, Mr. Romance Man."

He lowered his hands and glared at her, his eyes mere slits. "*My* game plan? As I recall, this anti-*Romance by the Book* gambit was all your idea."

Kathy hunched her shoulders and propped her forearms on the table. "I'm still in shock after you told me Quentin wrote that stupid book. Makes me even more furious watching Sailor fall for a complete phony."

"And of course there's nothing phony about you and me pretending interest in each other so I can be your date at all these literary functions."

"How else could I get you to the events so you could keep an eye on Sailor? You want to save her from herself as much as I do."

Kathy's words jabbed like a knife. Parker clenched one fist atop the table. "Save her from herself? No, that isn't what I want at all. I want her to *be* herself. I want her to be true to the person God created her to be." *Whether that includes me in her life or not.*

Kathy straightened, her gaze as intense as his. "I think we can agree God didn't create Sailor to be arm candy for Quentin Easley. And until she figures that out for herself, I refuse to apologize for manipulating circumstances until she does."

❧

Sailor barely made it home from Springfield in time for the Tuesday-evening committee meeting and drove straight to the library in the rented van. When she plunked into her chair next to Allan Biltmore, he apologized again for not being available to take Chandler and Quentin to the airport himself. "But of course we couldn't reschedule Nelda's appointment with her cardiologist."

"It's fine." Sailor flicked her breeze-tossed hair off her shoulder. "I was glad to get the chance to tell Chandler good-bye, but I'm very disappointed he has to miss his own awards ceremony."

Allan sighed. "At least Quentin can fill in for him. What a dedicated young man."

"Yes, Chandler's fortunate to have him." She opened her folder of notes and pretended to study them while the memory of Quentin's almost kiss behind the bookshelves last week played havoc with her concentration. If not for Kathy's timely appearance. . .

Since the book signing, she'd used every means possible to avoid being alone with Quentin. Even so, his subtle touches—caressing her cheek, stroking the back of her hand, nudging her toe under restaurant tables—suggested he'd like to be much more physical. Flattered as she was, she was also secretly terrified. When it came to relationships, *inexperienced* hardly began to describe her. How could a shy, small-town YMCA instructor ever live up to the expectations of a sophisticated, jet-setting New Yorker? It would take a lot more than designer outfits, spa treatments, and expensive haircuts to turn this missionaries' kid into a woman of the world.

"Sailor? *Ahem*, Sailor!" Donna DuPont's piercing tone finally captured Sailor's attention. "We're ready for your report, dear."

"Right." The meeting had started already? Emerging from her brain fog, Sailor fumbled through her notes as she explained about Chandler's unexpected departure. A collective moan filled the boardroom, until she added that Quentin would return to fulfill Chandler's festival commitments.

"Oh my, that's so good of him." Donna splayed her fingers across her throat. "What a blessing he must be to Chandler."

A muted growl sounded on Sailor's right. She shifted her gaze to see Kathy's tight grip on the chair arm. Obviously Kathy had transferred her negative assessment of Chandler's character to Quentin, and Sailor could only hope it was equally misplaced.

With the festival just over a week away, the meeting ran much longer than usual. It was after eleven when Sailor gathered up her things with a yawn and started out to the parking lot.

"Sailor, wait up!" Kathy cornered her next to the statue of a child sitting cross-legged with a book in his lap. "Want to have lunch tomorrow? We haven't shared any decent girl talk since Chandler came to town."

"I'm way behind on my desk work at the Y." She fanned away a cluster of bugs attracted to the streetlight above her. "Besides, wouldn't you rather see if Parker's free for lunch?"

"Parker? Oh, um. . ." Kathy shuffled her feet. "He's probably got appointments."

"Then why don't you take him lunch at the salon?"

Kathy shrugged. "We'll see. But if you change your mind, let me know."

Truth be told, Sailor would much rather have lunch with Kathy than catch up on paperwork at the Y. She'd never expected serving on the Bards of Birkenstock committee would turn out to be so involved.

Forcing a cheery good-bye, she marched across the empty parking lot to the rental van and slid into the driver's seat. By the time she picked up her own car at the Biltmores' and let herself into the darkened kitchen at home, exhaustion overwhelmed her. Uncle Ed had probably gone to bed hours ago. At least she'd have one full day of "normal" before Quentin returned and the prefestival activities resumed at breakneck pace.

She closed the bedroom door and sank into her desk chair to see if her parents had e-mailed. Moments after her poky old computer struggled back to life, the Skype chime sounded. She clicked the ANSWER icon.

"Hey, Sailor-girl!" A grainy video showed her father's smiling face.

"Daddy!"

"Your SKYPE button lit up, so I thought I'd catch you while I could. We haven't talked in ages." He squinted toward his

Webcam. "Is it the transmission, or are those dark circles under your eyes?"

"It's been a long day." She briefly described her unexpected trip to the Springfield airport. "How are you? How's Mom?"

"Your mother's still incommunicado while she oversees that new health clinic. It'll probably be her last one. The years are catching up with us."

"Oh, Dad." Sailor's stomach twisted. The worst part of having older parents—even worse than having them overseas most of her life—was realizing the time might soon come when she wouldn't have them at all.

And these days she needed a mother's advice more than ever.

They chatted a few minutes longer, until Sailor's father commented on her frequent yawns and told her to get to bed.

With sleep creeping in almost faster than she could change into her nightgown and brush her teeth, Sailor didn't waste any time. Lying there in the darkness, though, she felt an unexpected urgency to pray. She propped her pillow against the headboard, drew her knees up to her chest, and clasped her hands.

Dear Lord, please take care of my parents. I miss them and need them so much. And please help me know what to do about Quentin. His touch, his voice—he makes me feel things I never expected to feel. Yet I don't know whether I can trust my heart or not.

Especially when her heart kept whispering someone else's name. . .a name that slid through her lips on a sigh.

"Parker."

❧

"Have a seat, Gina. We're doing color and highlights today, right?" Parker flipped through his client file to verify the mix. Moonlit Mink #16, one of his favorites.

"I noticed my roots showing as I was getting dressed to go see Chuck—sorry, *Chandler Michaels*—at the book signing last week. Did you go?"

"Got there just before he left." He fastened the cape around Gina's neck and ran a brush through her hair. "The cut we did for you last time really suits you."

"Love it—so many compliments. You probably saw that tall, good-looking guy at the signing, the one who looks more like Chuck's book-jacket photo than he does?"

Parker took a slow, deep breath while he measured out the color and developer. "Quentin Easley. He's Chuck's assistant."

"He sure had the younger fans drooling. If I were single and ten years younger—"

Carla, the receptionist, skidded around the cubicle wall on the toes of her ballet flats. "Message for you, Parker."

"Thanks." He took the yellow slip from Carla and scanned the cryptic note: *Sailor working through lunch at Y. Think about it. Kathy.*

Carla folded her arms and shot him a knowing smirk. "Any response?"

"Uh, no. But you can do a couple of things for me. First, make sure I don't have any appointments over the lunch hour."

Carla's smirk morphed into a grin. "I already checked. You're free between eleven forty-five and one thirty."

She was too good. He'd have to give her a raise. "Then please call in an order to Audra's Café for. . ." He scanned his memory banks. "Make it two Asian salads with grilled salmon." Another memory flashed through his brain. "No wontons. And dressing on the side."

As he returned to his color mixing, he caught Gina's questioning look through the mirror. She wiggled an eyebrow. "Sounds like someone has a hot lunch date."

He simply smiled and retrieved his coloring brush. The more deeply he let himself fall in love with Sailor, the more uncomfortable he'd become with trying to manipulate her emotions. Bad enough having to watch Quentin playing on her heartstrings. Why should Parker risk confusing her with his own unimpressive attempts at romanticism?

Yet here he was, jumping at the chance to take her favorite salad over to her for lunch. He couldn't help himself. The idea of spending even a few minutes in her company bulldozed all reason from his usually logical brain.

He finished Gina's color and cut then hurried through two more styling appointments and a new-client consultation before he finally broke free shortly after eleven thirty. With two salads from Audra's Café in hand, plus chilled bottles of spring water, he strolled through the Y's sliding glass doors at five minutes before twelve.

The blond receptionist looked up from the front desk. "Can I help you?"

In the cubicle behind her he glimpsed a familiar blue-jeaned leg beneath a computer desk. The foot at the end of that leg tapped out a staccato rhythm—Sailor's typical show of frustration.

"I. . .uh. . ." His tongue stuck to the roof of his mouth.

"Mmm, I smell something from Audra's." The receptionist peered over the counter. "Did someone call in an order—oh, wait, you're not from Audra's. You're the stylist from Par Excellence. Sailor's water aerobics student, right?"

The toe stopped tapping. Parker's heart thumped harder. A split second later Sailor stepped through the opening. A bemused smile creased her cheeks.

"Hi, Parker. What are you doing here?"

He lifted the bag and grinned like a lovesick schoolboy. "I brought lunch."

❧

Pinpricks zinged up and down Sailor's limbs as she showed Parker to the Y's break room. She pulled out chairs at a round table next to the soft drink machine and moved aside the napkin holder. "This is so sweet of you."

"Couldn't stand the thought of you stuck here working through lunch." Parker set out the clear plastic take-out boxes and fished two utensil packets from the bottom of the bag.

"My favorite salad—I can't believe you remembered!" Sailor opened the container—no wontons. A thousand hummingbird wings fluttered in her chest. She started to thank Parker and then froze. "Wait. Aren't you supposed to be having lunch with Kathy?"

"What?" The confused quirk of his eyebrows suggested the idea hadn't even been discussed.

She studied him through narrowed eyes. Now that the initial surprise had worn off and her brain cogs had reengaged, nothing about Parker's unexpected arrival made sense. "And how did you even know I'd be here over lunch? The only person who could have told you is—"

Kathy!

She pushed her salad aside and draped one arm along the edge of the table. "Okay, Parker, what's *really* going on here?"

His lips mashed together in a crooked frown before he whooshed out a long breath. "Kathy left me a message this morning, saying you'd be working through lunch. The rest was all my idea."

"So. . .what's Kathy doing for lunch?"

"She didn't say." He cut his eyes sideways and then seized his plastic knife and began slicing through a hunk of salmon. "This is really good dressing. I like the spiciness. Is that the ginger?"

"Yes, ginger." Sailor popped the cap off the small dressing container—wait, dressing on the side? Yet another of her preferences Parker had remembered. And he'd made a special trip to bring her lunch when he could just as easily have done the same for Kathy. If he was here with her, and not with Kathy. . .

The thought that not one but two men had eyes for her sent her pulse rate skittering—and after all these years of thinking herself plain and unattractive. Once again a prayer rose in her thoughts. *Father, You know how long I've dreamed of meeting Mr. Right and being swept off my feet. Well, I've been swept—twice!—and now I don't know which way to fall. Don't let me make a mistake.*

The quiver beneath her breastbone made her wonder if Mr. Right might be sitting right in front of her.

sixteen

Allan Biltmore insisted on picking up Quentin at the airport on Thursday, which brought Sailor no end of relief. For one thing, she couldn't afford to cancel any more of her water aerobics classes. And for another, whenever she spent time with Quentin, she began to doubt her own good judgment.

The phone rang Thursday evening as she brushed a lemonteriyaki glaze over two chicken breasts for her and Uncle Ed's supper. Uncle Ed picked up and called her to the hallway phone. When he passed her the receiver, Quentin's mellow tones caressed her eardrum like a warm breeze.

"Hi, beautiful. I missed you. I can almost smell your perfume through the phone lines."

Something like an electric shock zapped her fingertips. She cast Uncle Ed a forced smile and motioned for him to set the chicken in the oven. Moving farther down the hall, she murmured into the phone, "I don't wear perfume."

"Then I'll have to do something about that. Hmm, roses? Jasmine? Citrus?"

"Quentin—"

"Jasmine, I think. Not too floral, not too spicy. Just like you."

Jasmine. . .like the heroine wore in *Love's Eternal Melody*. Sailor's breath snagged. Quentin sure knew all the right romantic buttons to push. Except. . .

"Really. I don't wear perfume. Gloria at the Y is allergic to scents, and it would wash away in the pool anyway, and—"

He chided her with a gentle *tsk-tsk*. "But you'd wear it for me, wouldn't you. . .when we're alone together? Sailor, I can't wait to see you again."

The sound of her name on his lips sent her stomach on a

roller-coaster ride. She could almost feel his breath on her cheek. "I'm looking forward to seeing you again, too." And at that moment she meant it.

"How about tonight? I'm locked in to dinner with the Biltmores, but we could go somewhere later for a nightcap."

"Quentin, I don't drink."

"Coffee then. A malt. A root beer float."

Laughter bubbled from her throat. His charm was quickly dissolving her defenses. "I can't. I already had one late night this week, and if I don't get my eight hours—"

"Don't you dare say you need your beauty sleep. I can't imagine you looking anything but drop-dead gorgeous."

"Then don't stop by the Y after one of my classes."

"Now you've got me curious. Don't be surprised if I show up tomorrow afternoon."

"Please don't." She covered her eyes with one hand, already cringing with embarrassment.

"Hey, I might need to sign up for one of your classes myself, just to see you in a swimsuit."

"Now, Quentin—"

Sailor felt a tug on her elbow and turned to see Uncle Ed standing behind her. "I don't know what to do with the vegetables."

"Be right there," she mouthed. Into the phone she said, "I have to go, Quentin. But I'll see you tomorrow evening. We have tickets to the Branson show, remember?"

"Oh yeah, Frankie what's-his-name. Jazz isn't my thing, but if that's what it takes to spend time with you. . ."

They said their good-byes, and Sailor's thoughts returned to Chandler. He'd been thrilled to learn the committee had arranged for him to see a Frankie Verona show. "I grew up listening to his albums," Chandler had said. "When I'm writing a romantic scene, nothing inspires me like one of Frankie's slow, sultry love ballads."

While she finished getting supper on the table, Sailor found herself humming one of the songs from Frankie's show last month. She pictured Parker onstage, lost in the soulful music of his flute. As she settled into her chair, a shiver jolted her.

Uncle Ed looked up from stirring sugar into his iced tea. "You catching a chill?"

"No, I'm fine." She smiled and unfolded her napkin.

"Well, it wouldn't surprise me, the way you've been dressing lately." Uncle Ed harrumphed and sliced off a bite of chicken.

"Just because I'm dressing a little more stylishly doesn't mean—"

"Pains me to think what your parents would say if they could see how you're flaunting yourself in front of that romance writer person."

"I am not flaunting myself, and there is absolutely nothing improper about my new clothes *or* my behavior." Her cheek muscles bunched. Uncle Ed seemed more out of touch all the time. "Shall I say grace?"

಻

"Hey, Grams, not doing so hot today?" Parker leaned over his grandmother's recliner and dropped a kiss on her forehead. She had to be feeling bad to miss one of Mom's weekend performances with Frankie.

"Must be a front coming through. I'm stiff as an old leather boot." Grams reached up a gnarled hand to pat Parker's cheek. "But you didn't have to waste a perfectly good Saturday evening to come sit with me. Shouldn't you be making time with that sweet little water aerobics instructor?"

Parker rolled his eyes and plopped onto the sofa, wincing as his back muscle went into spasm. He stretched his left hand around to massage the sore spot. If that "sweet little water aerobics instructor" didn't work him in for another practice session soon, he might have to move into Willow Tree with Grams.

"You know she was at Frankie's show last night." Grams adjusted the heating pad beneath her hips. "Would you hand me that afghan, please?"

Parker spread the pink and brown throw across her knees. "I heard the Bards of Birkenstock committee had reserved a block of seats. Kathy Richmond invited me as her guest, but I had to work late." Besides, he couldn't stomach yet another evening watching Quentin Easley cast his lecherous looks upon Sailor.

"It was not a pretty sight, let me tell you."

"What—Frankie's show?" Parker snatched a magazine from the coffee table. "I read this article on Billy Graham last week. Interesting."

"No, not Frankie's show, and don't change the subject. You know perfectly well what I'm talking about. I can't believe you're going to let some dude from New York City sweep that sweet little—"

"Grams, I get it. And I love you for caring so much." He tossed the magazine to the other end of the sofa and slid to his knees at the foot of her chair. Cradling one of her hands between his own, he stroked the swollen knuckles. These same hands once danced effortlessly up and down the keys of a flute, and it broke his heart to see how cruelly rheumatoid arthritis had abused them.

A sigh whispered between Grams's lips. "I only want you to be happy, son. You deserve to know a love like I had for your grandpa, like your mother and father shared." With a finger under his chin, she raised his head until their gazes met. "I know you feel a responsibility to look after your mother and me, but you have your own life to live. Besides, we're both pretty strong women, in case you haven't noticed."

"Headstrong, anyway." Parker released a chuckle.

"And planning to stay that way for a good long time." Grams's cheeks crinkled with laughter. "So stop wasting time. The Bible teaches us to 'number our days aright, that we may gain a heart of wisdom.' And God's wisdom tells us our lives are in His hands—every single part of our lives."

"I know, Grams, and I'm trying my best to trust the Lord." He pressed a kiss to the back of her hand and scooted onto the sofa. "But I can't force Sailor's affections. She has to choose for herself."

"Yes, but if you don't give her a reason to choose you. . ."

"I'm doing everything I can, but I can only be myself." Romance-meister or not, he couldn't change who he was to please Sailor any more than he'd expect her to change for him.

The problem was, Quentin Easley seemed all too persuasive in molding her into the woman *he* wanted her to be. And if he succeeded, the Sailor Kern Parker had fallen in love with might disappear forever.

❧

"I feel like I'm disappearing." Sailor stood before the mirror in the ladies' dressing room of Mabry's Department Store on Monday evening. A slinky black sequined cocktail dress clung to her slim figure.

Kathy stood behind her, two more dresses draped across her arm. "Don't talk like that. You look gorgeous."

"It's just. . .not me." Frustration choked her as she struggled to shimmy out of the tight-fitting garment.

"Hang on before you rip something." Kathy hung the other dresses on a hook and helped Sailor extract herself. Before Sailor could pull on her sweater top, Kathy grabbed the teal jersey calf-length dress and thrust it at her. "Oh no you don't. Like it or not, you've got to pick something for the gala. It's only five days away, or have you forgotten?"

"How could I?" With a groan Sailor stepped into the dress and slid her arms through the narrow sleeves. The higher neckline and longer hem made her feel less exposed, but the fabric hugged her curves—what few she had—almost as snugly as a swimsuit.

Kathy zipped up the back and peered over Sailor's shoulder. "The color's perfect, and I love the way the skirt flows out— makes you look like a ballerina. This is my favorite so far."

"You realize what all this shopping is doing to my budget. Why didn't you warn me being on your committee would be so expensive?"

The financial aspect was only the half of it. The closer they came to the Bards of Birkenstock Festival, the more she wondered what—*whom*—this whole experience was turning her into. While she enjoyed the new level of confidence gained from arranging first Chandler's and now Quentin's public appearances, she missed the predictable routine of her days at the Y. She missed the relaxing, if rather dull, evenings at home with Uncle Ed. .

Most of all, she missed dressing in T-shirt and jeans, swooping her hair up into a ponytail instead of worrying about blow-drying it correctly, and going bare-faced in public without feeling underdressed.

"I'm so sorry, Sailor." Kathy sank onto the narrow bench opposite the clothing hook. "I got you into this mess. It's all my fault."

Something in Kathy's voice snagged Sailor's attention. She sank down next to her friend. "No, *I'm* sorry. Here I am complaining when you handed me the opportunity of a lifetime." She squeezed Kathy's hand. "I got to meet Chandler Michaels in person!"

Kathy tipped her head in a sheepish grin. "He turned out to be a pretty neat guy, huh? I felt awful when I realized he had MS."

"His courage is inspiring. And his faith—he taught me so much in the short time he was here."

"I thought I sensed a change in you. What happened?"

Sailor's gaze swept the ceiling. "Nothing I can pinpoint. But when I saw how important his faith was to him, how fervently he worshipped, I realized what I'd been missing. More and more I've felt God's gentle nudges. It's like He's been with me all along, but I didn't want to let Him in, and now I do."

"That's great, Sailor." Kathy drew her into a one-arm hug.

"I think I'm going to cry."

"Oh, you!" Sailor pulled away and stood. "All right, Shopping Queen, is this *the* dress or not? It's nearly seven, and I still need to make a few calls tonight about Quentin's speaking engagements."

Kathy rose and studied Sailor from various angles. "Yes. Yes, this is the one. And you can wear those black stilettos you wore at the book signing the other night."

The mention of the book signing made Sailor's stomach roll. She pressed a hand to her abdomen and squeezed her eyes shut—a mistake, since the image behind her eyelids was that of Quentin's face looming above hers, his lips parted, his breath warm and tangy with breath-mint sweetness.

"Sailor? If you're worried about how much the dress costs—"

"It's not that." Sailor cast her friend a desperate frown. "Oh Kathy, I'm so confused. I wanted to fall head over heels in love with Chandler Michaels—or at least the man I imagined him to be. When I met him in person, I realized how childish I'd been. I was all ready to let go of those fantasies, until—"

"Until you met Quentin Easley." Kathy crossed her arms. "He's a hunk, no denying it, but. . ." She glanced to one side as if weighing her words.

"You can say it, Kathy. I know he's way out of my league." She pivoted. "Would you unzip me, please? I've really got to get home and make those calls."

"The truth is, *you* are way out of Quentin's league. He doesn't deserve you." Kathy exhaled sharply and slid the zipper pull down Sailor's back. "But there is someone who does."

Sailor squinted at Kathy from the corner of her eye. "What are you talking about?"

"I'm talking about the one man who's crazy for you, who's perfect for you, who loves you for who you are and not for who he could change you into."

A fizzy sensation swept from Sailor's knees to the top of

her skull. She gazed into the mirror, seeing not the tiny dressing room at Mabry's but a black and jungle green cubicle at Par Excellence Salon—and behind her the face of a smiling Parker Travis.

Reality returned, and Parker's image dissolved into the face of her friend Kathy. "Stop fighting it, Sailor. You know exactly who I'm talking about."

Sailor forced a swallow over the knot in her throat and remembered Parker's unexpected arrival with lunch last week. She turned to confront her friend. "But—but weren't you and Parker—"

Kathy pressed her hands to her temples and whooshed out a sigh. "All a sham. When Parker told me he had feelings for you, I started inviting him to be my 'date' at Chandler's functions so he could keep an eye on you and hopefully prevent you from falling for Chandler's romantic come-ons. Only now we're trying to protect you from Quentin instead."

Sailor didn't know whether to laugh out loud or storm from the dressing room in righteous indignation. Probably the latter, except here she stood with her dress unzipped and slipping down her shoulders. With a huff she squirmed out of the dress and snatched up her street clothes.

"Sailor—"

"Don't talk to me right now." She thrust her legs into her jeans and ripped the sweater top over her head while shoving her feet into her sneakers. *Protect me indeed!* Like she was a socially inept child without the skills to make her own character assessments.

Okay, so maybe the *socially inept* part was true, but hadn't everyone else been wrong about Chandler? Couldn't they be just as wrong about Quentin?

Oh God, help!

She started out the dressing room door then whirled around to grab the teal cocktail dress. Kathy was right—it set off her features perfectly, the ideal dress to make a knockout impression on the man of her dreams.

If only she could get it straight once and for all just who that man was!

❧

"We have to talk." Kathy stood at the entrance to Parker's station, arms folded and a worried frown creasing her mouth.

"I'm a little busy here, Kathy." He parted off a section of his client's damp hair, combed it straight up, and snipped. Something must have happened for Kathy to show up at the salon unannounced. The pinch in his gut told him it couldn't be good.

"I told her. Last night it all came out. All but the book, that is. I was ready to tell her about that, too, but she was so angry that she left before I had the chance."

Parker swallowed and tried to maintain his composure. He wasn't about to have this discussion in front of his church council treasurer. Neither could he leave his client stewing while he whisked Kathy to the break room for a private chat. "So. . .she knows you and I aren't. . ."

"Exactly."

The pinch turned into an all-out stomach cramp. He couldn't blame Sailor for being upset. The game playing had to stop. "Maybe I can talk to her. I have my class this afternoon."

"Good luck."

Parker made a point of arriving a few minutes early for his water aerobics class. If only Sailor would give him a chance to explain. He scanned the pool, where the three high school teachers and Miranda Wright were already warming up. He didn't see Sailor anywhere.

He knew this would be an even crazier week for her, what with the festival kicking off this weekend. Friday evening began with the Birkenstock Public Library hosting a reception and speaker panel featuring several prominent Missouri authors. On Saturday Quentin would stand in for Chandler Michaels as grand marshal of the annual festival parade through downtown. Parker had been hearing the Birkenstock High School band practicing its routine almost daily for two weeks now. Just about every school, club, service organization, and civic group in town would either march or decorate and ride on a float vying for the coveted Best in Show trophy.

Another book signing at Dale & Dean's followed in the afternoon, with all the guest authors autographing their books. Then the big event Saturday night—the gala dinner, silent auction, and awards ceremony.

Parker could hardly wait for the madness to end, but he worried how the sudden return to normalcy would affect Sailor. In the spotlight ever since Chandler's arrival, her confidence apparently at an all-time high and looking as if she just stepped out of the pages of *Harper's Bazaar*, would she come crashing down to earth when Quentin Easley flew off into the sunset?

Okay, so the sun set in the west and Quentin would be headed up east to New York. The end result would be the same. Parker couldn't picture Sailor ditching her small-town roots for big-city glitz and glamour to trail after the likes of Quentin Easley. And he couldn't picture Quentin staying faithful for long to a woman as pure and innocent and genuine as Sailor. Now or later, Quentin was bound to break her heart.

Parker only hoped he'd be around to pick up the pieces. . .if Sailor would let him.

Chirpy voices sounded behind him. He turned to see the Douglas twins sashay across the deck. *Wow.* He hadn't seen them in two weeks, and they'd slimmed down noticeably. No doubt they'd worked in the practice sessions he hadn't managed to. He smiled a greeting. "Hello, ladies."

"Hello yourself, stranger." Lorraine—at least he was pretty sure it was Lorraine—clutched his elbow. "Lucille and I were hoping to get appointments with you before the big doings this weekend. But I suppose you're booked up weeks ahead."

He hid a grimace. His schedule was already squeezed to

the limit, but he hated to turn anyone away, especially ladies like the Douglas twins who reminded him of Grams and her Willow Tree friends. Besides, the chlorine had really done a number on their perms, and he had a conditioning treatment he knew would help.

Rubbing his jaw, he mentally reviewed his calendar. He could easily work in a few evening appointments if he cancelled out on escorting Kathy to the rest of Quentin's prefestival appearances. Not much point in showing up for those anyway, now that Sailor knew the truth. And he wouldn't insult her with a big-brother-looking-over-her-shoulder routine.

With another quick look around the pool area, he turned to Lucille and Lorraine. "I just remembered I have a couple of cancellations. How about Wednesday or Thursday around six thirty?"

Lucille gave a squeal. "Oh, fabulous! Wednesday is choir practice, but Thursday would be *wonderful*!"

"Thank you *so much*, Parker!" Lorraine grabbed Lucille's hand and danced a little jig.

"My pleasure." He turned to follow them to the pool steps and found himself face-to-face with Sailor.

"That was nice of you." She tugged on the ends of the towel draped around her neck. "I guess that means you won't be at the library Thursday night. Quentin will be reading from Chandler's latest novel."

He rubbed the back of his head. "After what Kathy told me awhile ago, I figured you'd just as soon I didn't show up. Sailor, I'm sorry—"

"Apology accepted." She paused while the Douglas twins moved out of earshot. "I know you meant well. I just wish both of you would give me a little credit for being able to make my own decisions." Speaking so softly that Parker almost didn't hear her, she added, "You might even be surprised."

seventeen

With hardly a moment to herself all week, Sailor felt as if her head would explode. The pressure of constantly being "on" drained her both emotionally and physically. And to think, only a few weeks ago she'd been avidly looking forward to this weekend.

But that was before she met the real Chandler Michaels.

Before she met Quentin Easley.

Before she found herself torn between Quentin and Parker, the two most romantic men imaginable.

Although she doubted Parker Travis would consider himself the least bit romantic, much less on a par with Quentin. If only he knew how his soft-spoken ways and thoughtful attentiveness touched her heart.

Standing in front of the bathroom mirror, she manhandled a stubborn lock of hair around the styling brush and blasted it with the blow-dryer. Knowing Parker must have a full appointment list already—and especially after Kathy's confession Monday night—she hadn't felt comfortable asking for Parker's help getting ready for tonight's gala. Not that there would have been time. The autograph party at Dale & Dean's finally broke up around four, and the festival committee had been asked to be at the community center to oversee the setup arrangements no later than five.

Sailor checked her watch—nearly four thirty already! With a gasp she tossed aside the dryer and brushed her uncooperative hair into a ponytail. Parker had told her once how pretty she looked with her hair up. The memory evoked a tremor, but she couldn't afford to let her thoughts go there, not while this evening belonged to Quentin.

No, it really belonged to Chandler, and she would not let

herself forget that.

She pulled the ponytail higher, coaxed it into a few tendrils with hair spray and the styling brush, and fluffed her bangs. It would have to do.

In the bedroom she slithered into the teal blue cocktail dress and struggled to get it zipped. Then came the dreaded stilettos. She'd need foot surgery after wearing them for six or seven hours straight. Maybe she could find a few moments later to—

The doorbell chimed in the hallway. Surely not Quentin— they'd already agreed to meet later at the community center. Cracking her door a couple of inches, she listened for Uncle Ed to answer the door.

"Well, I'll be!" Uncle Ed let out a hearty laugh. "Ogden Kern, you are a sight for sore eyes!"

Sailor's stomach flip-flopped. *Dad?*

"Where's our girl, Ed?" Mom's voice. "Ogden's been a little concerned since he talked to her a few days ago, so once I got the clinic up and running, we decided it was time to come home for a while."

"Thank goodness, Hazel. I can't keep up with that girl anymore. She's in her room, getting gussied up for that big writer thing at the community center."

Oh no! What had she said to worry her dad that much? Sailor started out the door then remembered how she was dressed.

Too late. Mom's footsteps echoed in the hallway. "Sailor? Sailor, honey?"

She pasted on her most welcoming smile. "Hi, Mom! I can't believe you're here!"

Her mother froze. "Sailor Kern—that dress! And so much makeup!"

She felt five years old again, shamed into submission beneath her mother's disapproving frown. "I'm. . .going out. It's an important event."

"We've read all your e-mails about this literary festival you

were helping with, but you never said a word about—about—"
Mom sniffed, her hands fluttering up and down the front of her blue chambray shirtdress. "Thank heavens we came home when we did."

Sailor's father joined them in the hall, towering over them both. "Lectures can wait, Hazel. We haven't hugged our daughter in over two years. Come here, Sailor-girl."

Relieved, she moved into her father's open arms. His plaid shirt smelled of Old Spice and hours sitting on a plane.

"I wish you'd let me know you were coming. I have to be at the community center in half an hour."

Her mother shrugged her purse up her arm and offered Sailor a belated hug. "Of course we're glad to see you. But I never expected—"

"Please, Mom." She needed to placate her parents quickly and hope she could still get to the gala on time.

She drew her mother through the bedroom door and signaled her father to follow. Closing the door behind them, she pulled out the bench beneath her vanity while her parents seated themselves at the foot of the bed. "I'm dressed up because tonight is a huge formal event. But surely you know I'd never do anything to embarrass you."

"And what about yourself? Or the uncle who raised you all these years?" Mom straightened her shoulders. "Why, you're made up like a painted woman. And after all we tried to teach you about conforming to Christ's standards, not the world's."

Painted woman? Sailor closed her eyes briefly. Her foot tapped a frantic beat against the faded beige carpet. "You and Dad have spent most of the last forty years in third world countries. Uncle Ed stopped living when Aunt Trina died and keeps his nose buried in biographies about people who lived centuries ago."

She spread her hands and gave a helpless shrug. "But this is the twenty-first century. And this is the way people dress when they're going to a gala awards dinner."

"Perhaps we are out of touch with modern society," her

father said, his brows drawn together, "but in our minds you're still our little girl. The more we read your e-mails about spending so much time with this author person, and then your looking so tired and frazzled on the Webcam the other day, well, we're worried about you. The idea of your keeping company with a man who might want to take advantage—and you being so young and innocent—"

"Daddy, I'm not a child anymore." She reached for his hand, the sudden urge to cry tightening her throat. "I'm a thirty-two-year-old woman who's never even had a boyfriend. All I've dreamed about my whole adult life is to be seen as beautiful and special by a good man who loves me and wants to spend his life with me."

"Oh, Sailor, Sailor, honey." Mom rose and scooted onto the narrow bench next to her, pulling her against her side. "We want that for you, too. Your happiness is all we've ever wanted."

"It's why we left you in the States with Ed and Trina after you reached school age." Her father sighed and pushed his glasses up his nose. "They were younger, more stable. We thought they could give you a more normal life than you would have had traipsing to the farthest corners of the world with us."

"I know you did what you thought was best for me." A shaky sob tore through Sailor's throat. She rested her head on her mother's plump shoulder. "But I've missed you so much."

Mom patted Sailor's arm, her own voice choked with emotion. "Maybe it would've been better if we'd kept you with us after Trina died. You were at such a vulnerable age then."

"Now, Hazel, no use second-guessing ourselves. Sailor's got to get to her dinner. We can finish talking this out later." Dad stood and drew Sailor to her feet. "Let me get a better look at this fancy frock of yours. Why, the color's almost the same shade as your eyes. Mighty pretty, mighty pretty indeed."

Her father's compliment filled her with warmth. She cast a hopeful glance toward her mother.

Mom sighed. "You do look especially nice in that color, sweetheart. It's a lovely dress, very becoming." She used the side of her thumb to brush a tear from Sailor's cheek. "You'd best go fix your face, though. And all this hugging has mussed your hair."

Beaming, she gave her parents quick kisses and hurried to the bathroom. As she touched up her hair and makeup, she paused to thank God for giving her parents the grace of understanding. Halfway down the hall she stopped again, her heart brimming with unspeakable gratitude.

And thank You for loving me enough to bring my parents home exactly when I most needed them.

She couldn't wait for tonight to be over so she could introduce them to the man of her dreams—the man she realized she was falling a little more in love with every day.

☙

Parker hadn't worn a tuxedo since he'd stood up as best man in Andy Mendoza's wedding. The stiff collar chafed his neck, and those tiny studs that passed for buttons and cuff links gave him fits as he tried to manipulate them through their respective holes. But tie a bow tie? Forget it. With Mom down in Branson for Frankie's Saturday shows, he couldn't even ask her help.

He showed up on Kathy's doorstep ten minutes before five and held out the offending piece of black silk. "I should have opted for a clip-on, but the rental guy convinced me the real deal is classier."

"He's right." Kathy took the tie and ushered him into her living room, the full skirt of her black and silver waltz-length dress making soft swishing sounds. An aura of sandalwood surrounded her as she deftly worked the tie under his collar and shaped it into a proper bow.

Parker checked his reflection in the framed mirror hanging over the mantel. "Thanks. You look very nice, by the way."

"And may I say you look dashingly handsome, yourself. I'm

glad you decided to go as my escort after all." Kathy scooped up a lacy black shawl and satin evening bag. "I guess in a weird way we've kind of bonded over this Chandler Michaels thing. And tonight it'll finally be over. . .one way or the other."

Parker knew exactly which way he wanted it to end. He didn't want to think about the alternative—one more reason he'd convinced himself to attend the gala with Kathy. He had a feeling Quentin Easley would be pulling out all the stops tonight, the night when Sailor would be most beautiful. . .and most vulnerable.

The community center bustled with activity—technicians checking the sound system, caterers from Audra's Café carrying in chafing dishes and massive serving platters, wait staff arranging table settings, committee members checking the silent auction tables or adding last-minute touches to the decorations.

Kathy showed Parker to one of two large, round tables reserved for committee members, front and center below the dais. "Sailor will be at the head table with Quentin and the other celebrity authors and their guests. But at least you'll be close enough to keep an eye on her."

While Kathy hurried off to help as needed, Parker settled into a chair and strove for an air of nonchalance. A couple of other committee members left their spouses at the table, which meant Parker had to engage in the requisite small talk.

A bored-looking husband sat down next to Parker. "My wife's the literary member of the family. Give me a good baseball game on TV any day." He used his index finger to poke at the ice cubes in his water glass. "You a Cardinals fan?"

"I catch their games when I can." Parker watched the entrance for Sailor's arrival, while a distant part of his brain processed his companion's words. Parker had seen the affectionate kiss the man's wife had given him before she left to help with arrangements. They may have different interests, but the love between them was obvious.

I want that, Lord. I want it with Sailor.

Voices to his right made him look toward the dais. Quentin and several others in formal attire laughed and chatted as they found their place cards at the head table. Quentin sat down almost directly above Parker, an empty chair between him and the person to his left, a small, blond woman with an exuberant smile—probably another author.

Still no Sailor. Worry niggled the back of Parker's brain. He was about to go find Kathy when he saw Sailor scurrying between the tables. Intent on Quentin, she didn't even notice Parker, which gave him time to stare in silent admiration. The teal dress accented her slim figure to perfection, and the ponytail—simplicity at its best. The only jewelry she wore was a pair of teardrop rhinestone earrings. Anything more, especially on Sailor, would have been overkill.

As she took the chair between Quentin and the blond woman, Sailor's glance caught Parker's. She gave him a quick smile, ducking her head when Quentin slid his arm around her shoulders and drew her close for a kiss on the temple.

Parker did a slow burn. He reached for his water glass and hoped a cool drink would put out the fire long enough for him to get through the evening.

❧

"You look gorgeous, baby." Quentin's hot breath against Sailor's ear sent chills down her spine. "With you beside me, I'm the envy of every guy here."

The compliment made her heart sing. She cast Quentin a timid smile and tried not to look in Parker's direction. Knowing he and Kathy had only pretended to be dating, she hadn't expected he'd be here tonight. Truthfully she'd hoped he wouldn't. The thought of having Quentin lavish her with affection while Parker watched their every move made her feel like one giant blush.

At six o'clock sharp Donna DuPont stepped to the microphone and gave her welcome speech then invited the pastor from Rejoice Fellowship to come up and offer a blessing.

Returning to the microphone, Donna added, "Don't forget, the silent auction tables will be open until seven thirty, and we've had some outstanding donations this year. Keep those bids coming, because every cent goes to support literacy and the literary arts for our fair city."

The wait staff began serving dinner, and Sailor turned her attention to the sumptuous meal of rosemary chicken with artichoke hearts, prosciutto-wrapped asparagus, and rice pilaf. The chefs at Audra's Café had outdone themselves, and for once Sailor tried not to obsess too much about watching her diet.

When a server whisked away Quentin's empty plate, he crumpled his napkin and stood. He laid a possessive hand on Sailor's shoulder. "I need to step out for a bit. Care to join me?"

The thought of being alone with him made her stomach somersault. "No, thank you. I'm not finished with my dinner yet, and I see they're already bringing out dessert."

He bent closer, his fingers caressing the base of her throat. "Chocolate cake isn't exactly the dessert I've been hungry for." He started to leave then snatched up his wine glass. "Back in a few."

Sailor had barely a moment to stifle the tingles Quentin's touch had evoked before the blond woman to her left—an inspirational romance novelist from the authors' panel last night—nudged her arm. "That Quentin is a doll, almost as cute as my honey." She nodded toward the man at her left. "But what a shame Chandler Michaels couldn't be here. I was sure looking forward to meeting him. I love his books almost as much as my all-time favorite, *Gone with the Wind*."

"Yes, it's very disappointing." Reminded of Chandler, Sailor's heart dipped. She prayed he was doing better now that he'd returned home. Earlier, when she'd asked Quentin if he'd heard anything, she'd been slightly miffed to learn he hadn't made time to call and check.

Quentin still hadn't returned by the time Donna DuPont

announced the silent auction had closed. "And it looks like you've all done a great job of running up those bids. Our auction judges have given me a rough estimate of the total, and I'm thrilled to report we've surpassed our goal by at least three thousand dollars."

When the applause died down, Donna gave instructions on how the winning bidders should pay for and claim their items. "And now the moment we've all been waiting for—the Bards of Birkenstock Annual 'Best of Missouri' Author Recognition Awards. It's my pleasure to welcome committee member Kathy Richmond to begin the presentations."

While Kathy made her way up the dais steps, Sailor scanned the room for any sign of Quentin. Chandler's award wouldn't be presented until the very end, but it wouldn't look good for him to wander back to his seat halfway through the ceremony. She breathed a sigh of relief when she spotted him hurrying along the side wall. He slid into his chair as Kathy stepped behind the microphone.

Quentin scooted closer to Sailor and draped his arm across her shoulders. "Didn't mean to cut it so close. Wouldn't want to miss my—uh, Chandler's award."

She felt the heat through the fabric of his tux sleeve and wondered what he'd been doing all this time. "Is everything okay?"

"You reminded me how neglectful I'd been. I decided to give Chandler a call and see how he's doing." With a reassuring smile he grazed her cheek with a spearmint-scented kiss then turned to listen as Kathy announced the recipient of the Best Missouri Playwright Award.

Sailor forced herself to wait patiently while a short, bespectacled man approached the podium from the other end of the dais and gave a rambling acceptance speech. As he returned to his seat, Sailor angled her head to whisper in Quentin's ear, "How is he?"

Quentin cast her a confused frown. "Who?"

"Chandler. You said you called him."

"Right. He's better. Glad to be home and out from under all this pressure. Said to tell you hi and to stay in touch."

They sat through several more awards and speeches, until Kathy announced, "And now it's time for the moment we've all been waiting for, the introduction of this year's recipient of the Birkenstock Arts and Letters Association's Award for Outstanding Literary Achievement by a Missouri Author. Doing the honors is my very best friend and the newest member of the Bards of Birkenstock Committee, Sailor Kern."

As Kathy stepped aside, Sailor palmed the index card containing her speaking notes and stood, thankful her calf-length dress covered her trembling knees. Grinning, Quentin squeezed her hand and winked. Her pulse thundered in her ears as she moved to the podium. The microphone, set for Kathy, was about six inches too high for her. When she adjusted it, a loud, scraping sound blasted through the speakers. An embarrassed flush crept up her cheeks.

Discreetly clearing her throat, she set her notes before her and clamped her fingers around the edges of the podium. *"It's all about the persona. Act confident and you'll feel confident."* Such was the advice Josh Fanning had given her a few days ago. She spotted him and Deb a few tables away, and his reassuring smile helped calm her.

"G—Good evening, ladies and gentlemen. I can't tell you what a thrill it has been for me to spend time this past month with the recipient of this coveted award." Sailor glanced briefly at her notes, but as the words poured from her heart, she found she didn't need them. "Getting to know Chandler Michaels as a person, not merely a handsome face on the back of a book cover, has been an amazing experience. He taught me about courage, perseverance, and especially about faith through difficult circumstances. Meeting him made me realize that—literally—you can't judge a book by its cover. More importantly, we mustn't judge people by outward appearances, because what comes from the heart is what really makes us who we are."

The hall rang with applause, and Sailor took a few steadying breaths while she waited for silence. "That's why it gives me such great pleasure to present this year's award to Birkenstock's own Chandler Michaels—or, as many of you know him, Charles Michalicek."

More applause, accompanied with loud cheers as several in the audience rose in a standing ovation. When the applause subsided, Sailor went on, "Sadly, Chandler had to cut his visit short due to health problems. Accepting the award on Chandler's behalf is his assistant, Quentin Easley."

Kathy waited at Sailor's right with the engraved plaque, which Quentin stepped forward to accept. "This is truly an honor!" he said as he tilted the microphone to his level. "It broke Chandler's heart that he wasn't able to accept this award in person, but I know he's with us in spirit. Many of you know of his battle with MS, a battle he seems to be losing." Quentin gave a sniff and drew his hand across his mouth. "But I want you to know, the Chandler Michaels legacy will go on. His head is still brimming with story ideas, and I intend to do everything in my power to ensure that there'll be many more Chandler Michaels romances to come. I—"

Quentin stifled a choking sound with a fist to his lips. He gasped a few quick breaths and then lifted the plaque high, his gaze fixed on a distant spot in the rafters. "This is for you, Chandler."

As the hall once again filled with applause and cheers, Quentin turned to Sailor with a teary-eyed smile. "This got to me more than I thought it would," he whispered. "I need to get some air. Will you step outside with me?"

This time she couldn't refuse. His touching display of respect and affection for Chandler stirred something deep inside her and made her question her feelings for him all over again. She reached for the plaque and laid it on Quentin's chair. "There's a courtyard with some benches behind the building. I'll show you the way."

While Donna DuPont returned to the podium to close out the evening, Sailor and Quentin slipped out a side door. Pink-tinged streetlamps illuminated the path leading around the community center to the small park area. They found a white wrought iron bench beneath a stately oak. Nearby, a fountain burbled amid beds of deep purple irises and fragrant roses.

Quentin undid the button of his tux coat and tugged Sailor onto the bench beside him. "It means so much that I could share this evening with you, Sailor. Getting to know you these past three weeks—I hate to see it end."

She stared down at his hand entwined in hers, and her heart spiraled. Everything about Quentin oozed romance—the romance she'd always dreamed of. His sensuous glances, his silvery words, his seductive smile all conspired against her restraint. "I've enjoyed spending time with you, too, Quentin, but. . ." She slid her hand from his and inched away. "As flattered as I am by your attention, I've realized how little we have in common. And besides, you're flying back to New York tomorrow."

"All the more reason to make the most of tonight. I've never felt this way about a woman before. Sailor, you do things to me." He reached for her hand and placed it against his chest. "Feel that?"

His heartbeat thudded against her palm, sending shivers up her arm. Her own heart raced. She jerked her hand away. *Dear God, help me! I want this. . .and I don't!*

"What is it, Sailor? Are you afraid?" He chuckled softly and ran his fingers up and down her cheek. "You poor little girl, so naive, so inexperienced. I could teach you so much, if you'd only let me."

"Maybe we should go inside—" The words came out in a breathless gasp. She stood abruptly.

Quentin rose and swept her into his arms. "Not yet, baby. Not until I get what I came out here for."

"Quentin—" She struggled against him, sudden panic freezing the air in her lungs. His steamy breath on her face nearly choked her—the spearmint no longer camouflaging what she now realized was the smell of alcohol—something much stronger than a glass of dinner wine! The words from her own speech paraded across her thoughts: *"We mustn't judge people by outward appearances, because what comes from the heart is what really makes us who we are."*

And she now saw with painful clarity exactly the kind of man Quentin Easley was.

Cocking her elbows, she braced her hands against his chest and gave a mighty shove. "You're drunk! How could you, tonight of all nights?"

He spread his hands and shrugged. "How else was I supposed to get through those cheesy acceptance speeches?"

"The emotion you showed earlier—it was all fake, wasn't it?" She crossed her arms and huffed. "I didn't want to admit it, but the evidence has been in front of me all along. All those fans mistaking you for him, the way you bask in the attention while you autograph his books—you want Chandler's fame and glory for yourself."

"It was his idea. You can't blame me for taking advantage of the opportunity"—he stepped closer, a leering grin contorting his face—"or the perks that go with it."

Her fists knotted. She backed away. "Why you—you're not half the man Chandler is."

"You've got it wrong, baby. Admit it, I'm everything you dreamed *he* would be, everything you ever wanted in a man." His face hardened. "Come on, quit fighting it. You've been flirting with me ever since we met."

Flirt? She didn't even know how! "You're so full of yourself, you wouldn't recognize true romance if it bit you on the nose." Outraged, she started toward the building.

He lunged for her, snagging her skirt as she swiveled out of his reach. She yanked it out of his hand and tried to run, but he seized her arm. A strange, manic hunger lit a flame behind his eyes. His mouth loomed over hers.

"No!" She reached up with her free arm and landed a resounding slap against his cheek. When he flinched in surprise, she stomped on his instep with the heel of her stiletto.

He stumbled backward with a yelp. Darting down the path, she heard a splash and glanced over her shoulder to see Quentin sprawled in the fountain. While he sputtered and fumed and tried to extract himself, she kept running, her only thought a constantly repeated prayer: *Help me, Father! Help me!*

She ran headlong into a firm chest and sheltering arms and collapsed in weak relief.

৵

"You're okay, Sailor. You're safe now." Parker smoothed her mussed hair off her face and ran a soothing hand up and down her back while she struggled to catch her breath. The moment he'd seen Quentin hurry Sailor out of the banquet, his protective instincts had kicked in. He'd searched the lobby and anterooms until a guest said he'd seen the couple exit the building. Following the sounds of raised voices, Parker came upon the path to the courtyard, arriving in time to see Sailor break free from Quentin.

Her slim fingers clutched his lapels like talons. Something between terror and rage blazed in her eyes. "I should have known better. I'm such an idiot!"

"No, Sailor, Quentin's the idiot." Parker's own heart hammered with the urge to break a few of Quentin's bones. If he'd hurt Sailor, if he'd so much as—Parker couldn't even let himself imagine. *Thank You, God, for protecting her.* "Go on inside. Find Kathy and tell her what happened."

Quentin staggered toward them, his wet tuxedo plastered to his frame. "I don't know what she told you, but *nothing* happened." He scraped a hand through his dripping hair and released an ugly laugh. "See, that's the whole problem. Nothing ever would have happened. Sailor Kern is nothing more than a scaredy-cat little tease."

Hot rage exploded in Parker's chest. He gripped Sailor's shoulders and moved her behind him before stepping toe-to-toe with Quentin. "You couldn't be more wrong. Sailor is the purest, sweetest, most unpretentious woman I've ever met." Punching a finger at Quentin's breastbone, he went on, "You, on the other hand, are nothing more than a big phony, riding on the coattails of the real thing. You're a disgrace to Chandler Michaels, a disgrace to the literary world, a disgrace to the male gender."

"This, from Birkenstock's perennial-bachelor hairstylist?" Quentin's mouth spread in snide laughter. "I bet the whole town wonders why you haven't settled down with the right woman yet—or maybe they know you're just not man enough to handle a real woman."

Parker let the insult slide. The creep wasn't worth it. Clamping his lips together, he turned to take Sailor inside. "I think you should report this to the cops. He assaulted you."

"No, wait." An unreadable smile flickered across her lips as she gazed briefly into his eyes. Then she marched up to Quentin. "What you said earlier about my being inexperienced and naive—you're right, of course. I expected romance to be tender and pure, just like in Chandler's novels, and I wrongly assumed you'd be that kind of man."

She took a step back and slid her hand into Parker's, her gaze filled with warmth as their eyes met. "I should have realized that man was right here all the time."

Parker's breath lodged somewhere around his Adam's apple. He figured he must be grinning like a fool. "Just get out of here, Easley, or I really will call the cops."

Squishy footsteps confirmed Quentin's hasty departure, and Parker heaved a thankful sigh as he found himself alone— finally—with the woman he'd fallen in love with weeks ago.

He pulled her into his arms. "Are you okay?"

"I am now." She sucked in a shivery breath. "Did you mean

what you said about me?"

"I did. Did you mean what *you* said about me?"

"Every word."

"Sailor, I—" He drew her closer, his gaze sweeping the curve of her brow, the shape of her lips. "I don't think I can stand waiting a moment longer. Will you let me kiss you?"

♈

Sailor gulped and nodded. When his lips found hers in sweet, sweet ecstasy, she melted into his embrace. Her arms crept around him as the kiss warmed and deepened. A delightful languor spread from her core to the tips of her fingers and toes. It was everything she'd ever dreamed a first kiss could be—tender, sweet, gentle, insistent. How could she not have known, not have seen how much Parker cared for her? *Thank You, Lord, for saving me for this moment!*

Parker drew back with a shudder. "That was definitely worth the wait." He caressed the curve of her jaw, the corners of his mouth turning downward in a look of urgency. "I hope you know I'd never, ever hurt you. I love you, Sailor."

Her heart soared. She could scarcely find her voice. "I love you, too, Parker. I only wish I'd—"

As her hand slid down his tux coat, something protruding from his back pocket caught her wrist. Curious, she pulled the object from his pocket and held it to the light. *Romance by the Book: Tips and Tricks to Win Her Heart*—and the author was Chandler Michaels? Noticing the words *Advance Review Copy* bordering the front cover, she shot Parker a confused stare. "What are you doing with this?"

"Ammunition. Which, thankfully, I no longer need." He snatched the book from her hands and tossed it into the bushes.

"But wait—Chandler wrote that?"

"Not Chandler. Quentin." An exasperated breath whistled between his lips. "It's a long story."

Sailor shrugged and gave a half laugh. "Why do I have the feeling I really don't want to know?"

"There's only one thing you need to know: I'm crazy, wildly, madly in love with you." Parker swept her into his arms again and buried his face in her hair. "I may not be the most romantic guy on the planet, but I promise you, Sailor—if you'll let me, I'll spend the rest of my life learning how to make you happy."

"You already do." She snuggled against him and breathed in the crisp, starched scent of his dress shirt. "You already do."

epilogue

"Thanks for arranging for these tickets, Sailor." Chandler Michaels reached across the arm of his wheelchair and patted her hand.

She smiled from her seat in the handicap-accessible row. "Having connections with Frankie Verona's show musicians has its advantages."

Deb Fanning, seated on Sailor's other side with Josh and two of their sons, leaned forward and arched an eyebrow. "Something tells me those connections could get a whole lot stronger in the near future."

"Now, Deb!" Sailor crossed her arms and fixed her attention on the maroon velvet stage curtains at Frankie Verona's Moonlight over Missouri Theater. Knowing Parker was once again filling in for the flutist this weekend, she'd thought it the perfect time to bring Chandler to a show.

As if falling more in love with Parker every day weren't enough, Sailor could hardly believe her favorite author had moved back to Birkenstock over the summer—*and* hired her as his part-time assistant! Learning of the incident with Sailor following the awards dinner, Chandler immediately halted all plans to transfer his authorial identity to Quentin. He could no longer deny the truth—Quentin was a manipulative womanizer, out to use Chandler's fame for his own gain. Surprisingly, with Quentin out of the picture, Chandler's health seemed to stabilize, making him suspect the stress of trying to rein in Quentin's behavior had taken more of a toll than he realized.

The other good news was that Sailor's parents planned to retire at the end of the year and settle back in Birkenstock. Could her life be any more wonderful?

The familiar timpani fanfare preceded the announcer's voice:

"Ladies and gentlemen, welcome to Frankie Verona's Moonlight over Missouri Theater!" Sailor held her breath as the curtains parted and the music began. Spotting Parker, she beamed him a happy smile, her chest filling with pride as she watched him sway to the syncopated rhythms. She shifted her glance to Laura Travis standing with the backup singers and wiggled her fingers in silent gratitude for obtaining their tickets.

Each song seemed better than the last, and it warmed Sailor's heart to see how much Chandler enjoyed the show. Tilting her head toward him, she started to share an interesting detail about one of the band members when Frankie stepped to the front of the stage.

"And now, friends," Frankie began, "I have a very special song for you, one I recently cowrote with tonight's guest flutist, Parker Travis."

Deb nudged Sailor's arm. "How cool! Did you know about this?"

Sailor blinked. "I'm as surprised as you are."

Frankie motioned for Parker to join him at center stage. "You all know how I love romantic ballads, and this one, entitled 'With One Glance of Your Eyes,' is quickly becoming a favorite. It's inspired by Solomon's Song of Songs, the most romantic book ever written."

With a brief nod in Sailor's direction, Parker lifted his flute to his lips, and the whispery, evocative tones filled the theater. Chills danced up and down Sailor's arms when Frankie's mellow baritone joined in, creating a rhapsody of emotion in words and music. The song told of blossoming romance, hearts joined in harmony, God's love reflected in human eyes. When the song ended, silence blanketed the theater for a long moment before wild applause broke out. Sailor found herself swept to her feet with everyone else for a standing ovation.

"Thank you, thank you, ladies and gentlemen." Frankie bowed several times, as did Parker, until Frankie finally raised his hands to quiet the crowd. "House lights, please?" His gaze sought out Sailor, and he winked. "Miss Kern, would you join us onstage?"

The next thing she knew, two ushers were escorting her to the nearest steps. Frankie took her hand and bent to kiss it before leading her across the stage to where Parker stood. If Sailor didn't already know something was up, her suspicions were confirmed when Parker traded his flute for Frankie's microphone.

As Frankie sidled away, Parker dropped to one knee and reached for Sailor's hand. " 'Fair as the moon, bright as the sun, majestic as the stars in procession'—with one glance of your eyes, you've stolen my heart, Sailor Kern. I bless the day God sent you into my life. Will you marry me?"

Speechless at first, Sailor suddenly burst out laughing. "And you say you're not romantic!" She tugged on his hand until he stood, her gaze drinking him in while her heart soared far above the stage lights. A happy sob tore from her throat. "I can't imagine anything more wonderful than becoming your wife. Yes, I'll marry you!"

They shared a kiss beneath the spotlight, while a prayer of thanks rose in Sailor's heart. Over the past several months God had shown His love for her in so many ways, but none so beautiful as knowing one special man loved her just as she was.

A Letter To Our Readers

Dear Reader:

In order that we might better contribute to your reading enjoyment, we would appreciate your taking a few minutes to respond to the following questions. We welcome your comments and read each form and letter we receive. When completed, please return to the following:

Fiction Editor
Heartsong Presents
PO Box 719
Uhrichsville, Ohio 44683

1. Did you enjoy reading *Romance by the Book* by Myra Johnson?
   ❑ Very much! I would like to see more books by this author!
   ❑ Moderately. I would have enjoyed it more if

   _____

   _____

   _____

2. Are you a member of **Heartsong Presents**? ❑ Yes ❑ No
   If no, where did you purchase this book? _____

   _____

3. How would you rate, on a scale from 1 (poor) to 5 (superior), the cover design? _____

4. On a scale from 1 (poor) to 10 (superior), please rate the following elements.

   ____ Heroine   ____ Plot
   ____ Hero   ____ Inspirational theme
   ____ Setting   ____ Secondary characters

5. These characters were special because? _____
_____
_____

6. How has this book inspired your life? _____
_____
_____

7. What settings would you like to see covered in future
Heartsong Presents books? _____
_____
_____

8. What are some inspirational themes you would like to see
treated in future books? _____
_____
_____

9. Would you be interested in reading other **Heartsong
Presents** titles? ❏ Yes ❏ No

10. Please check your age range:
❏ Under 18 ❏ 18-24
❏ 25-34 ❏ 35-45
❏ 46-55 ❏ Over 55

Name _____
Occupation _____
Address _____
City, State, Zip_____
E-mail _____

MAINELY
MYSTERIES

Emily Gray stumbles into a rekindled romance and a trio of mysteries when she returns to the shores of Blue Heron Lake in northern Maine.

Fiction, paperback, 480 pages, 5⅜" x 8"

Heartsong

HEARTSONG PRESENTS TITLES AVAILABLE NOW:

(If ordering from this page, please remember to include it with the order form.)

Presents

Great Inspirational Romance at a Great Price!

Heartsong Presents books are inspirational romances in
contemporary and historical settings, designed to give you an
enjoyable, spirit-lifting reading experience. You can choose
wonderfully written titles from some of today's best authors like
Wanda E. Brunstetter, Mary Connealy, Susan Page Davis,
Cathy Marie Hake, Joyce Livingston, and many others.

When ordering quantities less than twelve, above titles are $2.97 each.
Not all titles may be available at time of order.

HEARTSONG
PRESENTS

If you love Christian romance...

$10.^{99}$

You'll love Heartsong Presents' inspiring and faith-filled romances by today's very best Christian authors...Wanda E. Brunstetter, Mary Connealy, Susan Page Davis, Cathy Marie Hake, and Joyce Livingston, to mention a few!

When you join Heartsong Presents, you'll enjoy four brand-new, mass-market, 176-page books—two contemporary and two historical—that will build you up in your faith when you discover God's role in every relationship you read about!

Imagine...four new romances every four weeks—with men and women like you who long to meet the one God has chosen as the love of their lives...all for the low price of $10.99 postpaid.

To join, simply visit www.heartsong presents.com or complete the coupon below and mail it to the address provided.